Vm3

Headed Str8t 4

TROUBLE

NICHOLE MARTIN

VM3: Headed Str8t 4 TROUBLE

Printed in the United States of America

ISBN-13:978-0692628324

ISBN-10:0692628320

Printed by Createspace 2016

Published by BlaqRayn Publishing Plus 2016

Vm3

Headed Str8t 4

TROUBLE

NICHOLE MARTIN

"SCARED AND CONFUSED"

SITTING AROUND THINKING OF SUCCESS

WHY IN THE HELL IS MY LIFE ONE BIG MESS

SO CONFUSED

MANY THINGS ON MY MIND

HOPEFULLY SOON THOSE TANGLES WILL

UNWIND

I still had an attitude the night he visited me. I opened the door and without giving him a chance to say hello or anything else, I quickly turned and walked towards the staircase, heading for my bedroom.

"BRING YOUR F^@%KIN' ASS BACK DOWN THESE DAMN STAIRS!" shouted El Creepo. Teddy and I both stopped just halfway up the staircase. Raising my left brow, I slowly turned to face the living room.

"WHO THE F^@% DO YOU THINK YOU'RE TALKING TO?" I shouted back. Grams and my mother suddenly exited their bedrooms.

"I'M TALKING TO THAT MOTHER#^@%*& THAT'S GOING UP THOSE STAIRS!" El Creepo was referring to Teddy.

"No you ain't BITCH!" I yelled as I opened my eyes widely.

"What's going on Nishi?" Grams asked, leaning over the banister.

"This idiot down here is gonna tell somebody, 'BRING YOUR F^@%KIN' ASS BACK DOWN THESE STAIRS' like he's runnin' shit around here," I explained.

"THAT'S RIGHT I SAID IT!" El Creepo boldly stated, continuing to talk his shit. "I'M TIRED OF SEEING HIS ASS GO UP AND DOWN THOSE STAIRS LIKE HE LIVES HERE."

"But this is her company," Grams calmly interrupted.

"YOU AT IT AGAIN MOTHER#^@%*&? DIDN'T ME AND EVELYN TELL YOU ONCE BEFORE THAT THIS AIN'T YOUR F#^KIN' HOUSE?" My mother angrily screamed as she slid her way down the staircase.

"F^@% YOU TOO!" El Creepo sneered, continuing to disrespect us.

"F^@% YOU! YOU SORRY BASTARD! WHATEVER GOES ON IN THIS HOUSE AIN'T GOT SHIT TO DO WITH YOU AND IF YOU DON'T LIKE IT YOU CAN GET THE F#^@ OUT!" my mother chastised him.

"GLADYS?" Grams yelled.

"WHAT?" my mother asked as she whipped her head around.

"From day one he's been talking his shit and you just let him go on with it. You better talk to your man!"

Like a nervous wreck, Grams went back into her room and moments later rejoined us with a glass of her favorite cognac (PINCH). The glass was only ¼ way filled – just enough to calm her nerves. By then Teddy had already gone into my room. As the three of us stood in the hallway discussing the recent situation, quickly and unexpectedly Grams ran into the bathroom. Although the door was closed, my mother and I could hear her passing loose stool. She always got the runs whenever her nerves were stirred up.

"So what do you have to say Mr. Lover man?" I asked as I entered my room and shut the door.

"Calm down," Teddy said, "'cause right now you're all upset and..."

"You damn right and your bullshit ain't helping it any either!" I interrupted him.

"Nishi come and sit next to me," he suggested.

"For what? I can hear you from here." I was sitting on my radiator near the window.

"Huhhh! All I have to say is that I didn't want you to find out, because I didn't want it to worry you," Teddy began to explain.

"So when were you going to tell me? Were you ever going to tell me?" I asked.

"Maybe one day," Teddy replied. "Listen Nishi…. as soon as I met this girl she got pregnant and nine months later I met you. I just wish that I had met you first, because me and she have nut'tin in common. We fight and argue every day and this was going on well before I even met you."

"Did you know her from back in Grenada?" I asked.

"I knew she family, but I didn't know she like that."

"So what made you date her in this country?" I questioned.

"Because when I got haye (here) - well, first of all my uncle sent me here after me first child was born," he explained. "He said I needed to do something else with my life other than make babies and then about a month or two after arriving in the U.S., I met up with Meryl."

"What do you mean you met up with her?"

"I saw she at a Grenadian get-together and from then on, we stat'tid (started) talking. I needed a place to stay and so I moved in wit (with) she."

"But didn't you tell me you lived with your sister when you first got here?"

"Yeah - I did, but once I stat'tid (started) wuckin' (working) she told me that it was time for me to get me own place."

"Oh," I smirked, "so that's where MooMoo comes in huh?"

"Yeah," Teddy nodded. "I wasn't straight yet, so me move in wit she, hoping to save up a little money to move on and she ended up getting pregnant some months later." Teddy hung his head and sadly shook it. "Believe me Nishi, I didn't want this gyul to get pregnant again."

"What happened to her diaphragm? Did it have a hole in it?" I sneered

"She stopped using it."

"Yeah - and you know why?" I snapped at him, "because when the BITCH found out that you were seeing me she wanted to trap you by having another baby. SUCH A SIMPLE BITCH! Is that how you people from Grenada are? Do you all lie and trick people?"

"Come and sit next to me," Teddy suggested again, while extending his hand to me.

I gave in this time, mainly because I was getting somewhat tired of arguing. He gently grabbed my head and laid it on his shoulder.

"I want you to stop riding that motorcycle too," he said, rubbing my belly. "You'll be six months soon. What if you fall or sum'tin (something)?"

"Please! I know how to handle myself," I snickered. "The wind blowin' against my face gives me the feeling of being free. The bike's much easier to handle cuz Sandra's not on it with me. Coming to a curve and leaning with the bike. The curvier the road, the more I feel the hype! The highway stretches are...."

"Nishi! Did you hear me?" Teddy interrupted, "I'm talking to you gyul! Stop riding that damn bike! Bet'tuh yet, you need to get rid of it!"

"Whatever!" I responded. *Damn fool. You just wrecked my flow!*

"I'm serious!" he grabbed my face and turned it so that I'd be looking directly at him.

I rolled my eyes at him. "Fine! Now get your hands outta my face... I don't know where they've been," I said, pushing his hands away.

_____

Juggling two women and undecided as to which one he'd commit to, he left at seven o'clock the next morning. I kissed him good-bye and watched as he descended the front steps to hop in his van, which was parked directly in front of the house by the hydrant. Instead of pulling right off, he sat as the van idled for about five minutes or so.

"WHAT ARE YOU WAITIN' FOR?" I shouted from the screen door, "PULL OFF ALREADY!" He continued to sit there, staring at me through his driver side window.

Whatever, I sucked my teeth. I closed the door and went back to bed.

Later that afternoon, Deanna and I took our little brothers to see the movie Batman Returns.

"Why is there so much glass in the middle of the street?" one of Deanna's little brothers asked.

"Maybe somebody broke a bottle or something," Deanna shrugged. Then she looked at me.

"Nishi wasn't Teddy's van parked there last night?"

"Yeah," I answered, not thinking much of her question.

"Well maybe he rolled over a bottle when he left," she assumed.

"Yeah maybe," I responded.

Now that the broken glass story was no longer our concern, we proceeded to the theater; the 1:30pm showing was soon to start.

"Lee sit down! You know better than to be jumping over the seats like that and you two big heads' back there - I saw you too. Don't jump over my seats again or else I'm gonna put you and your sister out and make all yuh Trini's walk to dee Plaza," I laughingly shouted to the back of the van.

"Shut up Nishi," Deanna's brothers smartly answered me back, "you're the one with the big head."

"Yeah, but not like yours," I began to laugh uncontrollably, "you two have heads like charter buses and those extra tight curls on the top ain't makin' it any better either. You mobile rugs' - stop jumpin' over my seats, sit your butts back and just shut up before I put you OUT!"

We returned home around 4pm. The sisters and brothers had experienced a fun filled day & it was now time for me to relax.

"NISHI!" One of our nosey ass neighbors was walking towards us and yelling my name. She and her mother WERE the block association.

"Nish I'll see you later girl. I'mma take my brothers inside to bathe and feed them." Deanna said, rolling her eyes. This was her way of eluding our very inquisitive neighbor.

"Alright - bye bus heads!" I smiled. Her brothers turned, giving me a smirk.

"What's up Nishi? Hey lil man!" Nosey, Jr greeted me and my brother.

"Hi," Lee answered then dashed inside the house.

"Girl, your belly is getting so big," Nosey Jr. observed. "Me and my mother saw you the other day on that motorcycle ridin' it as if you ain't pregnant. What's wrong with you?" *Oh here we go – the damn deputy is on the job.*

"Please - I can still have fun, I'm barely showing!" I said in a carefree tone.

"You know if the cops saw you riding, they could arrest you?"

"Well they won't be arresting me, `cause I stopped. Teddy doesn't like it either."

"Yeah - that's what I wanted to talk to you about."

"About what?" I frowned.

"Did somebody try to break into your boyfriend's van last night?" This was Nosey Sr.

"No."

"Are you sure?" she asked, "cause from my bedroom window I saw somebody banging on his driver side window. It sort of looked like a girl and she could have been pregnant too." *OH SHIT! That's where all that broken glass came from. MooMoo's crazy ass was over here! But who told her where I lived?*

"I wanted to say something to her, but by the time I got to my front door and opened it - she jumped in a cab," Nosey Jr. Explained.

"Well, I don't know anything about that. But I'll ask him if anyone broke into his van when I talk to him," I said, playing it super cool.

"I just wanted to let you know because this girl was banging on his van something fierce and some other girl was with her too," she continued.

"Alright, well let me go so I can get me something to eat. I'll talk to you later," I said, shutting her down. I was far from hungry but I HAD to get rid of her talkative, nosy butt.

"Ok girl, later," she said and took her private eye ass back down the block.

———————————

Sunday evening, Teddy called me.

"Hi swit'hat (sweetheart). How was you weekend?" he asked.

"It was okay," I replied. "Deanna and I took our little brothers to the movies."

"I was hoping that I had time to come and see you Saturday after me trip, but I didn't get back until two tut'tee (two thirty) this morning. I have two other trips to do next weekend, boat'a dem (both of them) are to Great Adventure. I have one on Saturday and dee ŭdda (other) one on Sunday. The lady that's giving the trip on Saturday said that she's gonna need two vans. You wanna do that one with me?" he asked.

"Yeah I'll do it," I agreed. "That's if my mother's not using the van to go upstate."

"Well you have to let me know for sure by next Friday, because if you can't then I'll have to find somebody else. I'm telling you first so you can have the chance to make a few dollars for you self over dee weekend."

"Okay - by next Friday," I confirmed. "But let me ask you this," I paused for a moment and took a deep breath.

"Hurry up 'cause I wanna go bathe and wash me hair," Teddy voiced. "It itchin' me muhn!"

"Don't rush me," I said.

"Come on gyul! What is it?" he said, growing annoyed.

"Did anyone break into your van on Friday night?" I blurted.

"No," Teddy answered quickly; a bit too quick!

"No?" I frowned. His rapid response sounded fishy.

"No," he reiterated. "Now let me go. I'll talk to you tomorrow."

"Okay – bye," I said and hung up.

"MOMMY! MOM-M-A-A-A-A-AY!" I shouted while running up the stairs.

"WHAT?" she answered from her room.

"Are you going upstate this coming weekend?" I asked.

"I don't know. From the way it looks, no. Why?" she asked.

"Because Teddy needs two vans for a trip on Saturday to Great Adventure and he asked me to work it with him."

"How much am I gonna get?" my mother asked.

"WHAT?" I asked in amazement.

"How much are they paying you?"

"I think it's like a hundred and eighty dollars," I replied, making a logical assumption.

"Well I want half of that," she requested. *WHAT? Is she serious?*

"But Mommy, I'm the one who's doing the trip," I said, rather disgusted that she would even suggest I give her HALF my damn earnings for a job she's not even doing.

"Yeah and you're using my van," she snapped. "That's wear and tear on my vehicle."

That foolishness almost made me not even want to do it, but that following Saturday morning, Teddy and I set out to pick up the two groups. They were all ready to go by the time we arrived.

"HEY! WE GOT A LADY DRIVER AND OUR VAN IS NEWER!" one of the teenagers shouted as the group boarded.

Some two and a half hours later, we arrived at the theme park.

"Now everyone listen up" the group leader yelled. "I want each and every one of you to be back at the vans by 9:00 pm. DID YOU ALL HEAR THAT? 9:00pm!"

"Nine o'clock? Why not make it ten when the park closes?" one teenager suggested.

"Because we want to be out of here by ten. Nine hours is enough for you guys," Teddy answered, speaking loud enough so the teenage crowd would hear him.

"That's right! We don't want to get caught up in the traffic on the way out of here, so 9:00, okay?" The leader ended her announcement then distributed the admission tickets. One by one the anxious teens headed for the park's entry point.

"Here Teddy - they only gave me one ticket for the driver. I told them that I had two drivers, but the clerk said that she could only supply me with one admission ticket - sorry."

"It's okay because she doesn't nǐd (need) to go in anyway," Teddy chuckled.

"Right! She won't be able to fit on those rides," the group leader added as she and Teddy laughed.

"Oh please, my belly's barely showin'," I snickered.

"Okay - I'll see you guys later." The group leader gathered her belongings and disappeared into the crowd.

The sole purpose of this trip for me was to make a dollar, so I truly could care less about getting on some amusement park rides; my bike was my ride and it was home waiting on me.

Shortly after the group leader left us, Teddy and I found ourselves relaxing in my mother's air conditioned van.

"Nishi I have something to tell you," Teddy sighed as he laid his head across my lap.

"What is it?" I asked, massaging his forehead to ease his headache. Teddy always complained of headaches and occasionally he'd take some Excedrin tablets to ease the pain.

"Remember when you asked me if someone had broken into me vahn and I told you NO?"

"Yeah," I said and patiently waited for him to continue on.

"Well that night someone did break me glass, but..." he paused.

"But what?" I removed my hand from his forehead.

"It was Meryl. She was in me vahn when I opened dee door to get in. She stayed in dee van all night and waited for me to come out of you house."

"How did she know where I lived?"

"She didn't. One of she friends tell she that one day they saw me vahn pa'hkd (parked) on 51st street and she decided to see for she self."

"Teddy I know all of this already because my nosy ass neighbor told me how it all went down," I smirked. "I just wanted to see how long you were going to go on with your lie."

"This gyul is so sickenin'," Teddy moaned. "She even call me mudda, way in Grenada, to tell she about you."

"For what?" I asked.

"I don't know. To me, she is makin' she self look stchu'pid because she whole family is in dee business now."

"And what did you say?"

"I tell Mommy that you is a nice gyul because Meryl told she all types of negative tings about you – tryin' to make you look bad," he admitted.

"And?" I prodded.

"And I just tell she and Mommy to lǐv (leave) me alone and to let me live me life. You see me – I'mma baldhead (one who has the Rasta mentality but without the locks)."

"Whatever! All I know is that I better not catch her on my block actin' crazy'!" I strongly expressed.

Throughout our conversation the van had gotten very warm, so I gave him the key to start it and to turn on the A/C, but before I knew anything, Teddy had taken off his clothes.

"What are you strippin' for?" I asked sarcastically. "The air conditioning works in this van."

"Yeah, I know. Take off you shŭt (shirt)!"

"No. Somebody might see us."

"Plĭz! (Please) Tru dese (through these) tints... dese windows are dăcker (darker) than me own (mine). Just take off you clothes gyul!" Teddy insisted.

Slowly I removed my shirt. One by one the cousins, the milk producers flopped out and my entire upper torso was exposed. The dairy queen was now ready to be milked. My bare breasts were instant gratification for Teddy. He knelt on the floor, raised my skirt and began to moisten my vaginal area. Now all this time I was thinking that I was going to be sucked elsewhere.

As the omnivore devoured his meal, I looked out to make sure no one was coming. As Teddy ran his tongue back and forth across the tip of my urethra, I laid my head back as he performed his oral wonder, but the second I allowed myself to embrace the moment -

BOOM! BOOM!

We both jumped up. Another carload of theme park guests had parked beside us and was unloading their vehicle. The brief interruption did not destroy the mood and so we reconnected, but this time around Teddy was sitting up on the chair. I performed fellatio as he caressed my lactating partners.

"I'm comin!" Teddy whispered. I eased up a bit. I didn't want to taste his liquid love again.

"Ummmm! I'm comin' Nishi!" he moaned.

I slid my lips to the tip of his fully erected penis and seconds later, SQUIRT! Although I backed away when I did, it still hit me in the face.

"F#^@%!" I squirmed and scurried to the front of my mother's van for some tissue.

"Bring more than one piss (piece)!" Teddy grunted.

As I returned to the rear of the van, he was kneeling on the seat, ready to go again.

"Lay on you side," he ordered. I followed his order and tried to lay on that narrow ass seat.

"WAIT! Teddy my back is hurting!" I said in discomfort.

"Alright - get on you nĭz (knees) then," he suggested.

I did as I was told and Teddy got behind me, entering me doggy style. Again, it was uncomfortable.

BOOM! BOOM! BOOM!

We raised our heads to see two of our passengers standing outside the van. Teddy jumped up and ran to the front as I got dressed.

"What's up?" Teddy asked the teens.

"Nothing," they said, side-eyeing each other, "we just forgot our swimming trunks." As they grabbed their belongings, Teddy and I fought to contain our laughter. Within seconds they were gone.

"See! I knew we were gonna get caught!" I hissed at him as he opened the windows to air out the van.

We quickly got dressed and, since we still had about another 6 hours before it was time for us to load up, we decided to have some fun inside the theme park too. Despite my ever-growing belly, I was able to enjoy a few rides with Teddy. We watched a few water shows and he won two large stuffed animals for me. He tried to win more, but a park employee noticed that he was on a hardcore winning streak and added his name to the "WINNERS LOG SHEET," withdrawing his privileges to play any more games throughout the park.

"Whatever!" I told the employee and pulled Teddy away from the stand.

Completely annoyed with the park policy, and feeling exhausted from the overbearing heat, we returned to the van, napping til it was time to go.

We arrived back in Brooklyn around 1:30 that morning. The trip had taken a lot out of me and I was tired as hell. We said our good-nights at the drop off site and went our separate ways. He had to get some sleep to prepare for yet another trip to Great Adventure later that day. This is the lifestyle of a man who fertilizes two eggs around the same time. He constantly works and gets all the coochie that he can eat. Teddy invented the buffet style...

Monday morning, I saw him on the road.

"How was your trip?" I asked as I rolled down my driver's side window.

"Alright," Teddy answered.

"Did you get any sleep?" I asked.

"Yeah, I slept in dee vahn."

"Ahhh - haaa! Your boyfriend slept in the v-a-a-a-n!" Robert sang.

"I'll talk to you later," I said and closed my window.

"Robert?" I watched him through the inside rear view mirror.

"Yeah Nishi?"

"Was anybody talking to you?" I snapped at him.

"No. But your...."

"Uhp! Uhp!" I interrupted him, "I don't wanna hear all that! I am just so happy that you brats only have one week left before school is out, 'cause you are..."

"Me too, 'cause ..." Robert interrupted me.

"Uhp! Just shut up!" I hissed. "I swear I've had enough of your damn mouth these past four years!"

I hadn't announced it yet, but this was going to be my last year of doing this school bus driving shit...

––––––––––––––––––

"Renee's in the hospital. She's been there since last night," Grams informed me later that afternoon.

"Did her water break?" I asked.

"No, but Paul called and said she's in a lot of pain." Grams explained. "She's not quite ready yet so the doctor instructed her to walk around the hospital to see if that'll help bring the baby down."

The next day I called to ask Paul about Renee' - to see if she had made any progress.

"Hello?" To my surprise Renee' was the one who answered the phone.

"Hey - I heard that you were in labor," I said to her.

"Please! As you can see they sent my black ass back home." Renee' irritably responded.

"Why?"

"Because I'm not dilating. The doctor said that maybe if I walk around it'll help bring the baby down. That's all I've been doing is f#^@%kin' walking and I'm tired. I walked around that entire hospital for five hours before they sent me home."

"Well, at least you know it's coming soon," I said.

"Yeah, not soon enough though," she said, sighing hard.

"Well - I'm gonna let you go, because I can hear the exhaustion in your voice. Tell Paul to call us if your condition changes."

"Okay, I will." Renee' promised.

"Later!" I hung up.

An entire week went by and Renee' was STILL pregnant.

"Yo Nish, pass by my job after you drop off the last kid, so I can pick up my check," Sandra requested.

Today was Friday and the last day of the school year.

"Alright Christopher, enjoy your summer!" I wished the kid well as he exited the van.

"Thank you!" he said happily as he jumped out.

"AJ?" I called to my little cousin.

"Yeah Nishi?"

"Come here fatty! Come sit up here in the front with me and Sandra."

"Okay." My rosy faced, chunky little cousin made his way to the front of the van. AJ was not only the first boy child in our family, he was my mother's only nephew, which is why it baffled me that she'd charge her own sister the same rate to transport him to and from school.

"If AJ rode with someone else then Evelyn would have to pay them, right? So why not pay me?" my mother responded after I inquired about AJ's transporting agreement one evening. *So wrong!*

In my opinion, this was not how family should deal with one another. But who was I to make waves? I was just an employee of an unregistered transportation business that

NEVER received any type of monetary compensation for my four years of dedicated labor.

"I wanna go to Bedford Avenue first," I told Sandra.

"No diggity. No doubt," Sandra responded.

Bedford Avenue was Teddy's hangout spot. I called it little Grenada. Every week it seemed as if another boat had docked and all of its passengers were placed on Bedford Avenue between Beverly and Cortelyou Roads.

As I drove down Bedford Avenue, Teddy's van was nowhere to be found.

"YO NISHI!" I heard someone yell. From my rear view mirror I saw a Rasta flagging me down something fierce, so I made a U-turn.

"Yo Nish, why are you turning around? I don't feel like seeing him now," Sandra moaned.

"Girl please!" I said. "Duck behind the seats then; he won't even notice you're in the van."

I pulled up in front of the refugee camp. Rumps stood grinning widely – as usual. The government must have given out some of that block cheese laced with cannabis earlier during the day.

"And AJ, don't let him know that I'm in the van either," Sandra said, squeezing between the seats.

"Shut up! He's walking towards the van now," I mumbled through my teeth.

"What's up Mrs. Ruthbun? What's up AJ?" Rumps greeted us. Ruthbun was Teddy's last name.

"Nothin' much. Oh so now I'm Mrs. Ruthbun huh – FUNNY!" I smirked.

"Please muhn! You were always Mrs. Ruthbun. From the day that I met you I knew this."

"Oh yeah and how's that?" I questioned him.

"Teddy may not talk much, but when he does I find out a lot. Believe me when I say that you're Mrs. Ruthbun."

Did Rumps know something I didn't?

"I can't tell, 'cause Ms. MooMoo is pregnant again," I reminded the Rasta man.

"Please, that gyul. I don't know about she. She and Teddy fight and argue all dee time, that's why he's always wit you. She told me never to come by she apartment again," Rumps explained.

"And I'm certain that's only because you took Sandra with you over there for Thanksgiving."

"That too, but she doesn't talk to me because she knows that I know the real deal about you and Teddy. She told Teddy to stop hanging around me because I was a bad influence. Ssssst, PLEASE! Teddy's a grown man and plus, he was dealing wit you before I even came to this country -

so that is she loss. So where's my gyul?" Rumps said, changing the subject.

"Who?" I asked, trying to sound dumb.

"What do you mean who?" Rumps asked, turning up his top lip. "Sandra. I know she rides wit you every Friday. Is she hiding in dee vahn?" He snatched open the side entry door and looked beneath the chairs.

"WHO TOLD HIM?" Sandra jumped up and shouted. "I KNOW THAT YOU TOLD HIM NISH!"

"No I didn't," I laughed, "he looked for himself."

"Sandra, you really tink (think) I don't know you?" Rumps laughed. "I passed down you (your) block dee udder (the other) day and saw you from a distance sittin' on you neighbors steps. When I stop to ask them if they had seen you, they told me 'no'. But here's dee ting (the thing) - I knew they were lying 'cause I saw you when you jump dee fence."

"Nah! I was looking for this kid's ball. He threw it over there by mistake," Sandra stumbled over her words, trying to cover it up.

"Yeah right! I know! But today I get to see you - tanks to my friend Nishi," Rumps said with a massive smile on his face AGAIN.

"Oh here comes you husband now,"

Rumps said looking to his left. Sandra and I turned and saw Teddy's van slowly approaching us. Any other time he'd be zooming down the streets as if he owned them. *Why is he creeping?*

"YO NISH, MOOMOO'S INSIDE THE VAN WITH HIM!" Sandra screeched as Teddy drove straight past me, double-parking the van some four cars in front of us.

"Are you sure? I didn't see anybody," I questioned her vision.

"YES-S-S!" Sandra voiced excitedly. "She's sittin' on the first row seat. I looked her dead in the face!" Rumps just looked on quietly.

"What the f#^@% is she doin' with him?" I was seething. I got out of the van and bravely approached Teddy. I could see him watching me through his driver's side view mirror.

"Hey Mr. Ted. Are you now finishing your run?" I asked while leaning up against his driver's side door.

"No. Me finish at 5 o'clock and den me went home to take a shower," he answered.

"You don't have to answer her questions!" MooMoo shouted from the back of his van.

"Why are you even here? Did you come for your ass kickin'?" I smirked.

"I came out with MY MAN!" MooMoo broadcasted.

"You lyin' gyul! You forced you self (yourself) into me vahn. I didn't ask you to come wit me… FŌ' WHAT?" Teddy blurted.

"YOU! SHUT UP!" MooMoo ordered him. She then reached forward and smacked Teddy on the side of his head.

"DON'T HIT ME GYUL! WHŬ DEE F#^@% IS WRONG WIT YOU? KEEP YOU HANDS TO YOU SELF!" Teddy yelled at her.

"YOU JUST SHUT UP AND DON'T TALK TO SHE!" she commanded.

"Why not?" Teddy asked.

"Because I said so!" she replied angrily.

This bitch was not only trying to control what Teddy did, but also what he said.

"Remember me MooMoo?" Sandra slyly approached the opposite side of Teddy's van.

"I don't care about you. All I know is that Teddy is MY MAN and I am 5 months pregnant wit he second child." MooMoo said while turning her nose up high with that annoying smug look of hers that was always present. I wouldn't call it a "face" because she was forever making herself look like an "ass".

"Oh yeah! Well your so called MAN must be something full, because he's been eatin' my pussy since we've met and still IS even though I'm SIX MONTHS PREGNANT! SO BITCH KISS `EM NOW!" I indecently shouted. When I said THAT everyone looked over at us… and I mean EVERYONE.

"WHAT! Boat'a dem makin' child?" (both of them are pregnant) A Grenadian bystander commented.

"Fuh troot?" (is it true) Another Grenadian bystander looked on in utter amazement.

"Oh gosh man – Teddy put he self in a big problem muhn!" the first bystander concluded.

First came the crazed look and then Meryl began to punch Teddy wildly. She obviously didn't see my protruding belly and I believe it was because of the thin jacket that I was wearing.

"HE'S NOT YOUR F#^@%KIN' CHILD SO WHY ARE YOU HITTING ON HIM LIKE THAT?" I yelled.

"I can do what I want to… he belongs to me!" She continued to flap her lips.

"No I don't!" Teddy frowned.

"BITCH! He already told you that he loved me. What more do you want? COME ON MY BLOCK AGAIN AND I'MMA F#^@% YOU UP!" I shouted.

"F#^@% YOU SLUT!" Meryl shouted.

"SLUT?" I frowned.

Somehow Teddy managed to get a bottle of Guinness Stout. I snatched the bottle from his hand and flung it at her. She ducked and the bottle itself missed her; however, the airborne Stout soiled her shirt.

"BITCH! GET THE F#^@% OUT OF THE DAMN VAN!" I shouted.

"SLUT! SLUT! YOU'RE JUST A SLUT!" Meryl screamed. "I WILL COME TO YOUR HOUSE ANYTIME I FEEL LIKE. ESPECIALLY, IF MY MAN IS DAYE (THERE)."

"If he is your man - then why do you have to come get him?" I challenged her.

"Can't you see that he doesn't want to be with you? The whole world knows this. Is that why you got pregnant again? So you can trap him? Is that how you keep a man

MooMoo – by trapping him? Why not try TRUE LOVE? Oh I forget - HE DOESN'T LOVE YOU!"

At this point, she was extremely pissed off and everyone could tell cause her arms were now crossed as she sat back and pouted like a big ass kid.

"YOU JUST HE SLUT!" That slut remark was getting on my nerves. It always did.

"Meryl why don't you just get out?" Teddy spat at her. The crowd looked on in amazement. None of us had expected for him to say such a thing.

"Yeah – get the f#^@% out!" Sandra repeated.

MooMoo continued to argue with him.

"Didn't you hear what YOUR man just said," I chuckled, teasing her, "GET O-U-T-T-T!"

I was waiting for her to set foot outside of that van so I could snatch that ass up.

"YOU STAT'TED (STARTED) IT, SO GET OUT!" Teddy yelled at MooMoo. "I'm tired of this shit! You big mout (mouth) got you in trouble now."

"I'm not getting out - I can't believe you Teddy." She looked as if she were going to cry.

"Believe him bitch and GET OUT!" I yelled.

We stood there for at least forty-five minutes waiting for her to get out.

"Nish, don't forget we still have AJ in the van," Sandra whispered in my ear. "Maybe we should take him home."

For several moments, I stood there thinking, waiting. To further add salt to Moo-Moo's wounds, I leaned into Teddy's van, gave him a deep, passionate kiss with lots of tongue, which he happily reciprocated, and rubbed his head, all while staring directly into MooMoo's eyes.

"I'll see you again bitch," I told her, smiling sweetly, then left with Sandra. We dropped AJ off at home and afterwards, swung by Renee's place.

"You're still here?" I asked as she opened her apartment door.

"Girl - I don't think this baby is coming any time soon and it's getting on my nerves too," Renee' complained. "Since that visit to the hospital I haven't felt any more labor pains.

"Word? It's probably a boy. They say boys are lazy like that," Sandra concluded.

"To change the topic, we just left from Bedford Avenue arguing with MooMoo," I sighed.

"For what?" Renee's spirit lit up.

"I was there waiting for Teddy to show up because he usually hangs there on Friday after the run."

"Okay?" Renee' said, trying to rush the story.

"Finally, he pulls up and to my surprise MooMoo was with him. He claims that she forced herself into his van."

"We should go over there," Renee' suggested. "I wanna see how she looks."

"Go where?" Sandra sternly questioned. "Your ass is in labor. You ain't going nowhere!"

"Please! I'm not having this baby anytime soon. So let's go! I'm gonna tell Paul that I'm going out for a ride," Renee' said, walking towards the rear of her apartment...

Some twenty minutes later, we were back on Bedford Avenue.

"Where is she Nish, can you still see her in his van?" Renee' asked as I pulled up directly behind Teddy's still double parked van.

"I see somebody movin', but I'm not sure if it's her," I answered. None of us could see through his tinted windows so we got out to get a better look.

"What's up Teddy?" Renee' said, looking throughout his van.

"Nut'tin', what are you doin' haye (here)?" he asked.

"Oh nothing, I just felt like getting out for some fresh air." Renee' obviously wasn't wrapped too tight because her belly had dropped and that baby could have come at any second.

"I heard that you had labor pains dee udder night," Teddy said trying to strike up a conversation.

"Yeah, but the doctor sent me home. They told me to do a lot of walking," Renee' said, leaning through Teddy's driver side front window.

"TEDDY TAKE ME HOME! I WANNA GO HOME!" MooMoo suddenly shouted.

"Why? You didn't want to go home before," Sandra said, standing on the passenger side of Teddy's van. The three of us had that van surrounded.

"Is that MooMoo?" Renee' asked, as if she didn't know.

"Yeah, that's her," I said looking over Renee's shoulder.

"SOMEBODY CALL DEE COPS! CALL DEE DAHMN COPS!" A Grenadian shouted.

"You want cops? Then why don't you call the damn POLICE!" Sandra told the individual.

He looked at her in disgust and walked away.

"TAKE ME HOME!" Meryl continued to shout.

Rumps and another one of Teddy's friends had now made their way over to Teddy's van.

"Renee' what you doing out here with that big stomach of yours?" Rumps smiled.

"Getting some fresh air," Renee' answered.

"Nishi just go home and leave it alone," Rumps said, turning to me, "because she's not going to get out of dee vahn."

"Yeah, but it was okay for her to come on my block and make a scene right? Having my neighbors all up in my damn business. YOU UGLY BITCH!" I shouted at her.

"SLUT!" she responded.

"Bitch, who you callin' a f#^@%kin' slut?" Renee' squinted at her.

"Your sister or whoever she is to you," Meryl answered Renee'.

"Just get out of the van. It's time for me to have my baby and I bet kickin' your ass will help bring it down," Renee' threatened.

"Go home! Nobody asked you to come here anyway," Meryl snapped at Renee'.

"Oh yeah?" Renee instantly walked away and in minutes, she returned with the crowbar from my mother's van. "Now bitch, who were you tellin' to go home?" Renee said while swinging the iron rod.

"CALL DEE COPS!" the Grenadian bystander shouted for the third time.

"SHUT THE F#^@% UP AND TAKE YOUR ASS INSIDE!" Sandra barked back.

As for me, I was the silent storm. I grew angrier and angrier as the clock ticked. I grabbed Teddy by his left arm to gain his undivided attention.

"Let me tell you one f#^@%kin' thing. You better get your shit straight, 'cause I am really tired of you and your bitch here. I will be having my baby soon and I'm not going to continue on with this bullshit. Do you understand what I am telling you? This shit has gone on for years and I'll be damned if I involve my child in it."

"I'll talk to you tomorrow okay - just go home and calm down and I'll talk to you later." Teddy spoke in a nervous tone.

POW!

Meryl hit Teddy on the side of his head again.

"You ain't callin' nobody tomorrow! You basodi? (Grenadian term meaning confused)?" MooMoo yelled.

"Gyul keep you f#^@%kin' hands to you self I said!" Teddy aggressively told her.

"See this shit - this is what I'm talking about. Why do you allow her to hit on you like this?" I asked him in disbelief.

"I can do what I want!" MooMoo continued on.

"This is my world. I don't know what you did in Grenada, but you are not gonna do it here." I said as I grazed Teddy's hand.

"Teddy, your hand's bleeding!" Renee' said frantically. He looked down and saw blood dripping everywhere. As he inspected his hand, I retracted the box cutter's blade then placed it back into my jacket pocket.

"Nishi why did you cut me?" Teddy asked almost in tears.

"Because I am tired of your shit! I wouldn't have been in this mix-up if you wouldn't have lied in the first place. I – TOLD – YOU – NOT – TO – F#^@% – WITH

ME, BUT IT'S TOO LATE NOW CAUSE I'M YOUR WORST NIGHTMARE!" I said as I clenched my teeth.

"You see, he's more scared of you than he is me," Meryl noticed. "And he should be," I scowled. "I live up to my promises."

"Nish let's go, 'cause somebody's gonna call the cops for real, now that he's bleeding," Sandra stated matter-of-factly.

"Here Teddy, you want some tissue?" Renee' had gone to my mother's van and returned with a hand full of napkins.

"Nishi, I'm out. I'll see y'all when you get home," Sandra started to walk off.

"SANDRA WAIT!" Renee' shouted.

"Nah, 'cause MooMoo aint gettin' outta the van and now that punk ass is bleeding...I'm out. Later!" Sandra continued walking.

"Nishi, Sandra's right. We came here to kick her ass - not to get arrested."

Without blinking an eye, I gave MooMoo one long stare then returned to my mother's van.

"Please - And I'm the last one that needs to be here. Shit! My ass is still on probation," Renee' stated, as she struggled to pull herself up into the van.

On July 24th, 1992, Renee' gave birth to a solid 9 lb. baby boy. He was the biggest baby I'd ever seen. He had a head full of curly hair and a nice rosy complexion. Gosh, he was beautiful!

"Did it hurt?" I asked Renee' while visiting her in recovery.

"Hell yeah it hurt!" she laughed. "I got twenty f#^@%kin' stitches in my ass to prove it!"

"Your turn now Nish," Paul smiled at me while cradling his son.

"Nishi, when the doctor told me to push, I shit myself," Renee' said, laughing.

"You're lying!" I replied, shaking my head.

"Nah, for real," Paul confirmed. "She really did coonse she self in front of all of us and I was like IL—L—L—L! I see it come outta she bee'tee hole (anus). The nurses washed it away quick though because they said that the baby could'a got sick if he would'a swallowed some of it, and then the next ting I see is she pat'tuh cake (vagina) open up WIDE. I was feelin' sorry for my boo. She looked like she was in a lot'a pain."

"LOOKED LIKE? I WAS in pain!" Renee' scowled.

"So Nish, you ready?" Paul asked.

"Please! I'm gonna push that baby out and the next day, I'mma be on my bike," I answered confidently.

"Girl you CRAZY! You always talking shite (shit). That baby is gonna kick YO' ass when it's comin' out. All I gots to say is that I hope it takes after the Maron's, 'cause DAMN! Teddy man, you straight up and down," Paul joked.

The entire room flooded with laughter. Paul was a husky guy and during Renee's pregnancy, they grew bigger together.

"Don't pay that fool any attention, he's just jealous. Most of his clothes are made with elastic in the waist." I rubbed Teddy's head, comforting him.

"JEALOUS? I tank (thank) God for givin' me some meat on me bones, but Teddy you still one cool ass bai (boy) though." Paul said, shaking Teddy's hand. Turns out that Paul and I had something in common after all. We were both big trash talkers, but the only difference was – I COULD BACK MINE UP.

"Leave Teddy alone Paul," Renee snapped in Teddy's defense. "You eyes pass (disrespect) dee mahn. He's not even sayin' anything. The man's just standing there minding his own business and you're talkin' pure shit - that's all you do."

"Teddy knows that I'm just jokin'. We all family here," Paul smiled.

It's true! Teddy wasn't as chatty as Paul, but Teddy's main reason for not responding to Paul's sarcastic remarks was because moments before entering the hospital, Teddy had taken several pulls from his already clipped joint.

"Ree, we're gonna be leaving you and your BIG family now. Do you know when you're going home?" I asked.

"Hopefully tomorrow morning. The doctor has to check me and I have yet to pass my first stool."

"Oh okay. I'll call to see if you're still up here and if I don't get an answer, I'll try you at home..."

As my due date approached, I grew somewhat anxious. However, I continued on with my active lifestyle. I jumped Double Dutch with some of the younger girls around the way and yes, I managed to sneak in one more motorcycle ride.

"Nishelle I don't understand. You're two weeks past your due date and yet, you haven't dropped nor shown any signs of labor. We're going to make this baby come," the doctor said during a clinical visit.

Just hours away from a scheduled induced delivery, on October 15, 1992, I gave birth to a healthy baby girl. My mother named her Sara; she was dying to name her first grandchild, so I allowed it.

Unlike Renee', my labor was only four sweet hours long. I cried like a baby when I heard the nurses say that my newborn was fine.

"The doctor said that I can go home tomorrow. Are you picking me up?" I asked Teddy one evening during visiting hours.

"I don't think so," he answered.

"Why not?" I frowned.

"Because - I'm tired."

"Tired from what?" I was becoming visibly agitated.

"Just tired okay," he said irritably.

"Did you put my carpet down yet?" I asked him, momentarily changing the subject.

"Yeah. Rumps helped me."

"What about the crib...when are you going to put that up?"

"I'll do it over dee weekend," he replied.

"So are you pickin' me up or what?" I asked him again.

"I already answered you."

"Whatever! I'll ask my mother then." *Asshole*! I had all the company in the world - my little blessing.

The next day he called me at home.

"Wah say?" (How are you?)

"Fine," I responded.

"How's me dottuh?" (daughter) Teddy asked.

"Fine."

"What time did you get home?"

SERIOUSLY? Negro stop questioning me PLEASE!

"Don't know."

"Nishi I'll talk to you later."

CLICK.

I hung up the phone and continued to unpack my overnight bag. Chew on my left cheek! You couldn't bring me home and now you wanna call and ask me a bunch of questions?

"NISHI YOUR BABY'S WAKING UP!" Grams yelled from the kitchen.

I quickly dropped everything and ran downstairs. Being that she looked so comfortable sleeping in the stroller, Grams and Granny Gladys babysat while I showered and unpacked my belongings.

"Nish, running up and down those stairs is no good for you. You may feel okay and think that everything's fine, but still, your body needs to rest," Grams advised.

I ignored her and continued to haul our Kirby vacuum cleaner up those stairs each time I saw a piece of lint on my new carpet. I took pride in my freshly painted bedroom. Everything was new and purple from the walls to the carpet. I just wanted everything to be perfect for my first born...

As promised, Teddy and Paul assembled the crib while Renee' and I exchanged labor & delivery stories that weekend.

"Nishi, the baby's crib is up. Come look!" Paul called me.

"Wow! That's nice Nishi. I know you spent a nice set of money on that, didn't you Teddy?" Renee' asked, gushing.

"Yeah. That's the one she wanted," Teddy answered.

Including the mattress, Teddy spent over five hundred dollars on my baby's crib. The entire set was white with two over-sized sturdy drawers at the bottom and attached to the head of the crib was a compartment of five small drawers; each drawer was decorated with gold colored metal handles. It was very stylish and made to last.

"After you put the bumper guard set on, it's gonna look real nice Nish," Renee' admired.

"Nish we're gonna leave now," Paul said. "It's getting late and the kids are gettin' sleepy."

"Okay," I nodded. "And thanks for helping Teddy out with the crib."

"Yeah muhn – tanks for dee help," Teddy concurred.

"No problem, anyt'ing for me cuz'zin Nishi."

"Teddy can you follow them out to make sure that the door is locked when they leave please?"

"Later Nish," Renee' said as she cuddled her bundle of joy, who was tightly wrapped up in his blanket. Tameera followed behind her daddy.

When Teddy returned to my room, he grabbed his coat.

"I'm lĭvin' (leaving) too," he said as he zipped it up.

"Fine," I shrugged my shoulders.

"What's wrong wit you gyul?" Teddy huffed. "You been actin' like dis ever since you had dee baby."

"BECAUSE YOU'RE FULL OF SHIT!" I screamed. "I CAN'T BELIEVE YOU DIDN'T PICK ME UP FROM THE HOSPITAL ON WEDNESDAY. MY MOTHER DIDN'T HELP MAKE THIS BABY. YOU DID F#^@% HEAD! THEN YOU HAVE THE NERVE TO GIVE ME SOME BULLSHIT LINE ABOUT BEING TOO TIRED!"

"I can't believe that you are still mad about that," he rolled his eyes and looked upward.

"Whatever!" I angrily stared at him.

"Okay Nishi, I was tired because you see the sĕhm (same) day that you were comin' home wit you baby..." he paused and looked away.

"I'm listening," Teddy had my undivided attention.

"I was in dee hospital wit Meryl. She was havin' labor pains and she had she baby that same morning."

"What?" I grimaced.

"She had she baby in dee same hospital and she room was next doe (door) to you own," he nervously explained.

"You asshole! Does she know that?"

"No, but dee nurse up daye (there) recognized me and asked me if she had seen me somewaye (somewhere) befo (before)? I tell she, Yeah. Me friend just had a baby too but she was in dee room next doe (door)."

"Did MooMoo hear this?" I asked.

"No. I was in dee hallway when dee nuss (nurse) stop me."

RING! RING!

"Shit! Teddy, answer that phone for me!" I quickly whispered hoping that the baby wouldn't wake up. Regardless of how nice her crib was, Sara didn't want to sleep in it. She'd cry whenever I lay her down in it.

"Hello?" he answered.

"Press the speaker button, but turn the volume down," I whispered.

"Teddy?" I heard Renee' say.

"Yeah," he replied.

"This is Renee'. I just wanted to know if the baby was sleeping in her crib."

"No. I'm still holding her," I managed to speak loud enough so that Renee' could hear me.

"Okay, I just wanted to know if she was sleeping in it. I'll call you tomorrow," she said.

"Okay, bye," I said and signaled for Teddy to terminate the call.

To eliminate some of the running up and down, I had the telephone company install a personal line in my bedroom.

"So what did she have?" I asked, picking up where Teddy and I had left off.

"A boy."

"Whatever! Anyway go home to your MooMoo, `cause you're making me sick right about now."

"Gyul, you need to relax. You just had a baby, so act like it."

"Bye Bitch Ass!"

This was supposed to be my time and the more he spoke, the more I grew pissed. Once again, MooMoo was screwing up the mood...

The next morning I called Renee' to fill her in. "Ree, you busy?" I asked.

"Nah, what up?"

"MooMoo had her baby," I revealed.

"When?" Renee' asked.

"Two days after I had Sara."

"Get the f#^@% out!" Renee shockingly voiced. "I thought you had her by at least a month!"

"Obviously someone miscalculated."

"That's some shit! What did she have?"

"Another boy."

"Teddy's gonna be busy for a while. Two babies at the same time, D-A-M-M-M-N!" she whistled.

"Eventually, I'm going to get rid of him," I told her. "I can't take this shit. I love him, but I hate him… know what I mean?"

"Girl, I know what you're going through… Paul is back to his old shit too," Renee sighed. "Every time I turn around, he's in Virginia. And he ain't no real hustler 'cause if he were then my mother wouldn't have been the one to buy my baby's crib for me…" She paused.

"…I'm not gonna front…when Sandra and your mother threw that shower for you, I was a little jealous. That fat bastard didn't do a damn thing for me, that's why I had to buy everything for JuJu myself." JuJu was her son's nickname.

"Where is he while you're talking that big shit?" I asked.

"In the streets somewhere. Wherever he is, I hope he's looking through the HELP WANTED section of today's paper 'cause fat boy needs a nine to five. That hustling shit ain't workin'," she said, sucking her teeth.

"So are you ready for your first day on the job?" I asked her.

"Yeah and your mother better pay me on time too," Renee huffed. "She's already talking shit. I told her that I want my two hundred and fifty dollars no later than Friday. Shit, I got a baby to feed and unlike you, I don't work for free."

The employer and her new employee were already bumping heads.

"Well, have fun 'cause that's one job I'm not gonna miss. I'll call you during the week to see how things are going."

"Okay, later Nish."

On Wednesday morning, exactly one week after Id given birth to Sara, something went terribly wrong. Approximately 1:30 a.m., I got up to feed and change the baby. When I pulled back the sheets to get back into bed, I realized that my linen was stained. I changed my padding and with a small towel, proceeded to scrub the soiled area. As I applied more pressure to the area, I felt an oozing sensation. Quickly, I returned to the bathroom and to my surprise the maxi pad was saturated with blood.

"Mommy!" I entered her room.

"Mommy wake up!" I forcefully shook her. The blood was now running down my leg.

"What?" she muttered.

"I'm bleeding and it won't stop."

"What?" she asked, still groggy from sleep. "It's gonna be a while before the bleeding stops Nish."

It was obvious she didn't comprehend the severity of my condition.

"No. I mean it's running like water." She quickly jumped up and followed me to the bathroom.

"Shit! How did this happen?" she frantically questioned me.

"When I got up to feed the baby, I realized I had a small blood stain on my sheet."

"Let me get Grams." She hurried down the hallway and knocked on my grandmother's bedroom door.

"What's going on out here?" I heard Grams say as she opened her door.

"Nishi's bleeding like a stuck pig. Watch the kids while I rush her to the hospital," my mother commanded while getting dressed.

"Bleeding?" Grams frowned.

"Yeah. The shit's drippin' like water," my mother explained.

"Oh my God! Gladys call the ambulance!"

Grams said with tremors in her voice and to the bathroom she ran.

The ambulance arrived within fifteen minutes. By then I had gotten dressed and made my way down to the living room.

"Miss can you walk?" One technician asked me.

"I can, but every time I move more blood rushes out," I explained.

"Okay, I want you to stand up for me." He pulled me up slightly by one of my arms.

"IT'S COMING DOWN! I CAN FEEL IT!" I screamed.

"CARRY HER OUT!" Grams yelled.

"Slowly! Just take one step at a time miss." The other technician instructed.

"Lord. They gonna let the girl bleed to death!"

Grams cried, holding her night gown together. As we reached the bottom of the stairs and slowly approached the rear of the ambulance, my mother turn towards the house.

"TAKE CARE OF THE KIDS GRAMS!" she shouted just before getting on board.

"CALL ME AND LET ME KNOW WHAT'S GOING ON OKAY?" Grams shouted back from the screen door.

"YEAH!"

"How old is she?" The technician asked, strapping me to the stretcher.

"Twenty one," my mother answered.

"Has this ever happened before?"

"No. She just had a baby last Wednesday."

"Were there any complications?" The technician took notes.

"No," my mother answered.

"Was it a full term - normal delivery?"

"Yes."

"Which hospital did she have the baby in?"

"Downstate."

"We're taking her to Kings County's Emergency room okay?"

"Yes," my mother agreed.

Moments later, they rolled me into the hospital.

"Mommy, can you call Sandra?" I asked.

I knew I was in grave danger and just wanted those who truly cared about me to be there.

"Okay and I'm gonna look for Wasobi too," she said. Wasobi was serving as an intern at several hospitals and Kings County just so happened to be one of them.

"Ms. Maron, I'm the emergency room nurse and I would like to draw some blood from you to get the lab tests going okay?" The nurse stated, already holding the necessary supplies in her hand.

I was too nervous and somewhat weak to say anything, so I simply nodded my head, authorizing her to stick me.

After collecting three tubes of blood, the nurse left me alone on the stretcher in a room filled with strangers. As I lay staring at the ceiling light, my body began to shiver and I could feel some wetness on my lower back area.

"Nish!" Sandra came running over to me. "Your moms called and told me that you wanted me to come down here...something about you bleeding. What happened?"

"I got up to feed the...." I started out.

"Yo, she called Teddy too?" Sandra interrupted me.

"I don't know why?" I asked.

"Cause, I see him at the door. The guard stopped him. I don't think he's gonna let him in though."

About twenty seconds later, Teddy approached my side. "What's up?" My baby's daddy and my best friend greeted one another simultaneously.

"What happened, the guard didn't wanna let you in?" Sandra asked him.

"No. He tellin' me some sheet (shit) about dee room being too crowded!" Teddy explained loudly.

"YO F#^@% HIM! HOW WOULD HE FEEL IF HIS FAMILY WAS IN THE EMERGENCY ROOM?" Sandra shouted as she looked in the guard's direction.

"Be quiet! Y'all givin' him a reason to put you out," I spoke easily to prevent the blood from gushing out.

"What happened?" Teddy asked.

"I don't know. I was just asking her that when I saw you at the door." Sandra and Teddy both looked down at me.

"I got up to feed the baby, and when I went to lay back down I realized that I was bleeding," I explained.

"Is it a lot of blood?" Sandra asked.

"Yeah. I was standing over a bucket and it was dripping like water. I changed my pad and it was full before I could reach my room." Teddy pulled the elastic part of my skirt down to take a look.

"You see anything?" Sandra asked too frightened to look.

"Yeah muhn it's a lot! She whole panty is covered in blood." He slowly released my skirt. The unpleasant look on his face caused me to worry.

"DAMN! WELL WHAT ARE THEY WAITIN' ON?" Sandra yelled throughout the room.

"The nurse took three tubes of blood from me and just left me here," I told them.

"Why are they taking blood from you and you're losing it all the while?" Sandra asked me.

"Excuse me!" In my peripheral, I saw Teddy approach the nurses' station.

"Yes, are you with Ms. Maron?" I heard a woman ask.

"Yes. I'm she boyfriend. Can you tell me what's taking dee doctors so long to see she?"

"There are seven people ahead of her and plus, we have to wait until her lab results come back." The nurse explained.

"And how long is that gonna be?" Sandra turned towards her and asked.

"About two hours," the nurse answered.

"TWO HOURS! ANYTHING COULD HAPPEN WITHIN THOSE TWO HOURS." Sandra and Teddy started to argue with the nurse.

"Isn't this supposed to be the emergency room?" Teddy asked.

"Seven people before her. THAT'S BULLSHIT! Did you even check to see how much blood she's losin'?" Sandra screeched.

"These f#^@%kin' people up in haye stchu'pid muhn (here stupid man)!" Teddy stated loudly.

"You two are making way too much noise. Come on! You're gonna have to leave."The guard escorted them out.

"DON'T TOUCH ME! I'M LEAVING!" Sandra shouted.

I lay there watching them and the clock through a window. An entire hour had passed and still I hadn't seen a doctor yet. My back began to hurt and I was now shaking excessively. *Oh my God! Why am I shaking like this?*

"Nurse!" I yelled as loud as I could.

"Nurse! The girl on the stretcher is calling you," someone in the waiting room yelled.

The nurse quickly ran over and leaned over me.

"Yes, what is it Ms. Maron?" she asked.

"My back hurts and I'm very cold," I told her.

"My God!" her eyes widened. "What's taking these doctors' so long back here? I'll be right back," she stated, quickly walking away.

All I could do was watch Sandra and Teddy through that window and wonder. Minutes later, that same nurse returned and instead of leaving me there in the waiting room, she pushed me around to the back.

"I don't know what's taking so long, but if something happens to you they're not going to blame me. You're next okay?" she said, pushing my stretcher closer against the wall.

"Doctor this young lady here is next. She gave birth exactly one week ago and now she's bleeding heavily." The nurse briefed him on my condition. The doctor then pushed me into the examining room.

"WOW! You are losing a lot of blood. How long were you bleeding like this?" the doctor asked.

"Since 1:30 this morning," I answered.

"The nurse said that you had a baby."

"Yeah. Last Wednesday."

"Did you have any complications?"

"No."

"Was it a vaginal delivery?"

"Yes."

"Did your doctor give you an episiotomy?"

"Yes."

"Okay - I'm gonna push down on your stomach now, just relax."

Gently, he applied pressure and I could feel the blood gushing out.

"You feel any better?" the doctor asked.

"Yes," I nodded. My belly had gone down significantly.

"I know you do; a clot the size of a baby came out. From my experience, it looks as if the doctor left a piece of the placenta inside of your uterus and it seems to have gotten infected," the doctor explained. He then inserted his fingers inside of me to examine my uterus.

"Yeah, that's exactly what happened and you still have clots inside of you. I'm going to send you up to the third floor. Up there, they'll perform a D.N.C. This way the remaining clots will be removed and hopefully, it'll stop the bleeding. From what I can see, the episiotomy area is healing well which only tells me that the bleeding is coming from inside only."

The doctor maintained his composure throughout the examining process, but I could tell from the slight frown on his face that he was grossed out from the sight of all that blood.

"Nurse!" the doctor yelled as he removed his surgical gloves.

"Yes, I'm coming," she answered.

"This patient is going upstairs for a D.N.C. Where's her chart?" he asked her.

"She doesn't have one. I'm still waiting for her blood work to come back."

"Can you get me a chart for my patient please?" he impatiently stated.

"I'll write one up for you right now." She quickly exited the room.

"I don't know what's wrong with these nurses today. If you can't handle the E.R. environment, then go work in a clinic. That chart should have been prepared from the moment you came in," the doctor explained to me.

"Okay here you are doctor and her blood work just came back too," the nurse stated as she re-entered the room.

"Thank you. And can you change her linen please? It's sopping wet."

"Ms. Maron, I already told your family that you would be going up to the third floor, so they're waiting in the hallway for you," the nurse informed me as she cleaned me up.

"Can they go upstairs with me?" I asked.

"Sure. There's a waiting room up there also."

She covered me up then wheeled me into the corridor. Upstairs was totally different. There was no movement, just those long airy corridors.

It was sort of spooky.

"Doctor this is Ms. Maron. She was brought to the emergency room via ambulance at approximately 2:00 this morning and has been diagnosed as a post-partum hemorrhage," the nurse briefed the third floor physician.

"Has she had any blood work done?" the doctor asked.

"Yes. Her results are in the chart," the nurse said as she released my stretcher.

"Okay Nishelle, my name is Dr. Stevenson and I will be performing the D.N.C on you this morning."

In the background I could hear the emergency room nurse talking to my family, expressing her sincere wishes for my speedy recovery before returning to her post.

"According to your lab results, you've lost a significant amount of blood and you'll need a blood transfusion," Dr. Stevenson informed me.

"MOMMY!" I yelled. The word transfusion terrified me.

"What happened?" My mother came running. Sandra and Teddy were just two steps behind her.

"Your daughter has lost a lot of blood and is in need of a blood transfusion."

"She lost that much blood?" My mother asked in amazement.

"Yes, and she really needs it," Dr. Stevenson sternly replied.

"Can I take the blood from my family or my boyfriend?" I asked.

"No, because we don't have time to test it. It takes six months to test a donor's blood. Can you wait for six months? No. You can't!" the doctor solemnly voiced.

Tears began to roll down my face.

"Then let me go!" I cried. Teddy held my hand and began to rub my head.

"There's no other way?" Teddy asked the doctor.

"No there isn't. And if we delay this procedure, it will only complicate your situation," the doctor looked down at me.

"Mommy take care of my baby please. Teddy please don't forget Sara,"

I cried as I began to face reality and said my good-byes.

"No Nish. Don't give up!" Sandra grew worried.

"This procedure is about an hour long, so I'll be asking you all to leave momentarily. She's going to be admitted and you all can come back and see her later on during the day. I'll give you a few minutes with her and when I come back you'll have to go," Dr. Stevenson said then left the room.

I looked up at Teddy and tears were rolling down his face. I squeezed his hand indicating that I really didn't want to go this way, but neither did I want a blood transfusion. He knelt down and rested his head against mine.

"Nishi you'll make it. You a strong gyul. You have to lïv for you dottuh (daughter)," he said.

"Just do what you have to do to get better and we'll take care of Sara. Just focus on getting better, okay baby?" my mother said.

"Nish... Oh my God! Nish!" Sandra couldn't talk for crying. Dr. Stevenson re-entered the room.

"Okay, you can come and see her later. Go home and get some sleep - we'll take care of her from here."

The images of my family slowly faded away as they exited through that airy corridor.

"Nishelle. I want you to sit up. The nurse and I will help you remove your clothing and get into this gown. Now I'm not going to lie to you; this procedure is a little painful, so I'm going to administer a local anesthesia. This will eliminate some of the pain. I'll let you know when I'm about to start because I don't want you to move. Everything has to come out or you'll continue to bleed and the transfusion will no longer be an option." As the doctor spoke, I simply stared into space, remembering my daughter's beautiful round face and her baby scent.

"I know you're scared, but don't worry you'll make it. This doctor knows what she's doing!" The nurse assured me as she prepared to run my I.V.

"Nishelle. In a few seconds you will feel a burning sensation. This is simply the anesthesia running through your veins. You will start to feel sleepy, but you won't fall asleep. Again, this is just to help eliminate some of the pain. Are you with me?" Dr. Stevenson asked. I nodded yes.

"You're doing fine. I'm going to turn the machine on now. It's a little noisy, so don't make any sudden moves. I'm tired and I'm sure you are too. If we cooperate with one another it will be over before you know it."

CLICK!

She hit the switch. The machine sounded like an enormous vacuum.

"You're gonna feel some pulling. What this machine does is suck out the remaining clots which are causing the hemorrhaging." During Dr. Stevenson's explanation, the nurse grabbed my hand.

"I'm with you," the nurse said. "Squeeze my hand! It's okay. That's what I'm here for."

CLICK!

The machine was now off. As I lay on that stretcher with my knees bent and legs spread widely, I felt a tug.

"I'm just adjusting the speculum a bit. I wanna make sure that it's situated where I can get everything out so we don't have to do this again."

The room was cold and dimly lit. My legs began to quiver.

"No! Don't shake!" The doctor voiced firmly as she increased the pressure of the machine's nozzle.

Not only was I weak and cold, but with her constantly moving that instrument around inside of me, it made things worse. Lord, please let this be over soon.

"Squeeze my hand Nishelle!" The nurse instructed. I'm assuming she saw the uneasiness on my face.

"It's cold!" I mumbled.

"You're cold because you lost a lot of blood." The nurse said.

"A lot is coming out, but I want to get it ALL!" Dr. Stevenson shouted over the loud suction noise.

My legs felt like they weighed a ton and I just wanted to relax them.

"Okay," she said, turning the machine off. I slightly lifted my head and saw a tall container filled with blood.

"Relax Nishelle! The anesthesia is still in your system and you're not going anywhere any time soon, so just relax. You'll be here with us for a couple of days," Dr. Stevenson advised as she removed the speculum.

"Right now I'm going to wash away the excess blood with a solution called Betadine."

SWOOSH!

She doused my vaginal area with the cold liquid.

SWOOSH!

She did it again. I started to shake once again.

"Okay, I'm done here," Dr. Stevenson concluded. She removed her surgical gloves then turned to wrap up the machine.

"Nishelle, how are you feeling now? Better?" Dr. Stevenson asked me.

"Yes," I answered drowsily.

"Good and I know that you're tired too – just as myself, and as soon as I'm done with this paper work I'm going home to get some rest as well. The nurse is going to clean you up real good and then she's going to move you up to your room. I'll be back later this afternoon to check on you."

She said and exited the room.

At about 8:30 that same morning a nurse woke me up to take my vitals.

"104°. You have a fever. I'll be back with some Tylenol."

She laid her portable thermometer on the bed next to my leg. While waiting for her to come back I scanned my surroundings. Separating me from the other patients were dingy curtains and other sick women were everywhere.

"Okay, here's your Tylenol. We have to bring your temperature down because if not, the doctors' won't let you go home," the recovery room nurse stated. She was much older than my first two nurses.

"Won't let me go home - for real?" I asked.

"Yes. They're very strict about that. Usually when the patient has a temp over 101°, that's a sign of an infection. Are you still bleeding heavily?"

"I'm still bleeding, but it's not that heavy."

"You still have time. The doctors like to give patients like a day or so before the bleeding totally subsides. When did you have your D.N.C done?" she asked.

"This morning around 4:00," I answered.

"Yeah, you still have time. Hopefully, by tomorrow morning your temp will have gone down."

I pulled the sheets up to cover myself.

"No, don't cover up! You'll stay running fevers. Just keep drinking lots of liquids and in four hours I'll check your temperature again." Before the nurse left my side she added another saline solution to my I.V. drip then drew the curtain closed.

In no time, I went back to sleep...

"Nish?" I subconsciously heard.

"Nish." *There it goes again.* I batted my eyes.

"What's up? How you feelin'?" My friend 'til the end was hovering over me.

"I'm okay. What time is it?" I asked her groggily.

"12:15pm."

"Did you go by the house?" I slowly began to sit up.

"Nah, but I called your moms to see if she knew what time the visiting hours started. She didn't know, but what she did say was that your brat kept your grandmother up all night," Sandra laughed.

"I'm back to check your temperature." The nurse said as she pushed the I.V. pole aside. Sandra took a few steps back to give the nurse her space.

"Okay, it's gone down some, but we still have work to do because it's still a little high. See?" She leaned over to show me the digital reading.

"102.4°. We can definitely do better. Let's get those liquids down," she said, then moved on to her next patient.

"Yo, Teddy was at the house when I called over there. Your moms said he came straight after he finished his morning run. She said he made some type of drink that's supposed to build your blood." Sandra pulled up a chair and took a seat.

"Oh Lord. Some concoction from Grenada. What about Renee`? How's she makin' out with the school run?" I asked. Despite my fever, I was feeling much better; better enough to carry on a conversation.

"Oh, I don't know. But I do know Renee' bought the van back late. Your moms said Renee' is probably using her van to run her personal errands. Then she said that it's okay 'cause she's just gonna dock her pay at the end of the week."

"I can see Renee` is gonna enjoy working for my mother." I stated pessimistically.

"For real, 'cause your moms is a trip," Sandra shook her head in disbelief.

"Hi Nishi." Someone slowly pulled the curtain back. It was the man of my dreams.

"Hi," I happily replied.

"What's up Sandra?" Teddy spoke while placing a plastic bag on my portable stand.

"Wus up Teddy?" Sandra responded.

"Hey sweetie how you doin'?" He walked over and kissed me on my forehead. Ahhhh! His Chanel scented cologne soothed me.

"I'm okay, but I have a fever and the nurse said usually that's a sign of an infection."

"Did you stop blĭddin' (bleeding)?" Teddy then asked me.

"I'm still bleeding, but it's more like spots. Not heavily."

"That's good! At least it's not heavy. Nish, you remember when the guard put me and Teddy out?" Sandra asked.

"Yeah."

"Well we didn't see you through the window, nor did we know that the nurse had taken you to the back, so I went back in that room to look for you," Sandra began to explain.

"Okay. But wait a minute! You walked passed the guard?" I looked her dead in the eye.

"Hell yeah! F^@% him!" She huffed. I shook my head in disbelief.

"Well anyway, there was this girl waitin' to see the doctor too and she asked me if I was lookin' for you. I told her yeah and then she told me that they took you in the back. Now there was this other chick who was obviously listening in on our conversation.. she pointed to a puddle of blood and said 'that's where your friend's stretcher was."

"Was it a lot?" I asked.

"Yeah mun!" Teddy joined in the conversation.

"Hell yeah! It was all over the floor," Sandra said, shaking her head. Teddy began to rummage through the bag he'd brought in.

"Look! I měd you sum'tin (made you something)." He unscrewed the lid of the container.

"What is it?" I asked.

"Roots gyul! Roots! Here drink it!" He put it to my lips.

"Wait – Hold up! Where did you make this? I hope not at your house, `cause if you did you know I'm not drinking it," I argued.

"Gyul shut up nuh and drink it!" he ordered.

"For real! I'm not joking. Where did you make it?" I asked again.

"At you house gyul!" he sucked his teeth and placed the jar of serum back at my mouth. I took a sip.

"What is this stuff supposed to do?" I asked.

"Build you blood. Now drink up!" he tilted the jar.

"So Nish, did the doctor say that you still needed a blood transfusion?" Sandra asked.

"I haven't seen her yet and even if she did, I'm still gonna decline. Like I said, just take care of my baby."

"Stop talkin' like that. You're gonna make it I told you. As long as you it (eat) and drink the right foods, you'll be fine," Teddy said.

"Are they giving you iron up in here?" Sandra asked.

"Yeah," I answered.

"Alright. Just checkin'. Yo where's the bathroom?"

"Girl. You're asking the wrong one. I use the bed pan. Here, you can use it too if you want."

We all laughed. I was sick and still I had my sense of humor.

"Let me ask the nurse." She headed for the nurses station.

"When I left dee hospital this morning. I cried like a baby. I was hopin' they didn't give you a blood transfusion," Teddy stated.

"Did MooMoo ask you what happened?" I asked him.

"She was dee one who answered dee phone when you mudduh (mother) called. She talk she shit while me get dress, but I tell she to leave me alone and then left. I couldn't belĭv (believe) it when I heard you mudduh say that you was bahk (back) in dee hospital."

Teddy spoke sincerely. There was no smell of rum on his breath nor the scent of weed coming from his clothes. He was drug free and for the moment, his words were coming straight from his heart.

"I'm gonna lĭv (leave) soon because it's almost two tut'tee (two thirty)." If only he had a substitute driver.

"Have you seen Renee` out there?" I asked.

"Yeah, me see she yesterday. She hahn'lin' (handling) dee vahn (van) okay. I just hope she doesn't bang it'tup like all'yuh did dee orange vahn. That reminds me, I have to change dee oil and dee brakes on you vahn. It's been mo' dan (more than) six munts (months) since I did those brakes and I'm sure they need changing now," he said.

Not only was Teddy my part time lover, the mechanic, my mother's smoking partner and my baby's daddy, he was now "our" everything.

"Damn! I had to walk down that LONG ass hallway just to go to the bathroom," Sandra said as she drew the curtain.

"No - don't close it. I'm lĭvin' now," Teddy said.

"Oh you leavin'?" Sandra asked releasing the drapes.

"Yeah, it's almost time for me to do dee afternoon run. I'll see you later okay," he kissed my forehead. "And finish dee roots!" He added.

"I will," I promised.

"Later Sandra."

"Alright – alright," my best friend nodded, acknowledging Teddy's exit.

"So I guess Meryl knows that you're in the hospital by now?" Immediately, Sandra hit me with questions.

"Yeah, Teddy said she started bitchin' right after my mother called there, but WHATEVER! She'll get over it."

"Yep. Yo, I can't believe they got all of y'all bunched up in this one big ass room like this. When I got off the elevator I asked a nurse at the nurses' station for your room and when she pointed in this direction I was like, *yo chick, where the hell are you sending me to?* Shit, I thought this was the cafeteria," Sandra joked.

"This is how it is when you have Medicaid," I sighed, shaking my head. "I thought I was going to have a private room as well. Especially, after I heard the doctor tell the nurse to clean me up and take me to my room. I had no idea that I'd be in a room full of bloody asses. "

"You got jokes Nish," Sandra laughed.

"You see that one over there?" I pointed across the room.

"Yeah - what about her?"

"She had a miscarriage and the one across from me had a hysterectomy."

"What about the one next to you?"

"I don't know. She was there when I woke up."

"How do you know all this?" Sandra asked.

"Because I can hear everything during their examinations. So yeah, this IS the cafeteria and they're only serving fish. Haaaa!" I continued to tell jokes.

"You got mad jokes. Finish drinkin' your roots, `cause we want your blood to build up so you can get the hell outta here!"

"Get out of here is right and right about now I need to go to the bathroom," I mentioned.

"Are you supposed to be getting' outta the bed?" Sandra asked.

"Yeah - you see the nurse that just passed us?"

"Yeah," Sandra looked to her left.

"Well, she told me that I should get up and try to walk around."

"Oh alright, let's walk then," Sandra agreed. I tightened the lid on the jar and placed it on the table.

"Okay Sandra, when I say pull, slightly pull my arm so I won't have to put too much pressure on my back."

I extended my arm to her and took a deep breath.

"Pull!" With Sandra's help I was able to completely sit up and swing my feet over the edge of that bed.

"Be careful with the I.V. Nish!" Sandra said as we inched our way out of the ward; baby steps are all I could take.

"We have a LONG walk Nish. You see where that [Exit] sign is? That's where we gotta go," Sandra pointed out.

"I'll hold on to the I.V. pole while you hold my gown together at the back. This ain't the Playboy infirmary you know. I don't want everybody glancing at my ass, especially with these over-sized pads on. If only Teddy could see me now – he would never yam (eat) this again," I chuckled.

"I don't know about that. At the rate he's makin' babies nowadays, he might. You're still talkin' a lot of shit for someone who's sick," Sandra said jokingly as she crept behind me.

"I'm sick, I ain't dead. Sandra my legs..."

"NURSE!"

I heard Sandra scream then seconds after, everything turned into one big blur. Only two minutes on the floor and I was already sliding down the pole. Maybe this was the Playboy infirmary after all.

"SOMEBODY BRING ME A CHAIR OR SOMETHING! SHE FAINTED!" Sandra yelled for help.

"Where was she going?" I heard someone ask.

"To the bathroom," Sandra answered.

"She needs to stay in the bed. It's too soon for her to be walking around. What would have happened if you weren't here? She could have fallen and hit her head on this hard floor," the nurse explained.

This of course wasn't the same nurse who suggested that I walk around. They wheeled me back to the Presidential Suite, placed me back onto my Sealy Serta posturepedic next to the newly admitted caviar. She couldn't have been no more than 15 years old – a baby...

––––––––––

Two days after the procedure, I was sent home with three prescriptions. A multi-vitamin (once a day), an antibiotic (twice a day) and of course, one for iron (three times a day with two refills).

I recovered quickly which is why I was able to strike many poses. Six months later, my flat tummy and hourglass figure was back.

BAMMM! I lost all my weight, plus a few extra pounds. I exercised and did crunches every day.

Without having to ask, Teddy dropped off a case of baby formula, pampers and baby wipes one afternoon. He played with Sara for a quick minute. Afterwards, he went missing for DAYS. At the time, "Seven Whole Days" by Toni Braxton was a hit song. Each time it played on the radio, I'd sing it word for word, growing upset because it reminded me so much of my topsy-turvy love life.

"Heylo," she answered the phone.

"Can I speak to Teddy please?" I asked politely.

"He's not haye (here)."

"Thank you."

CLICK!

I hung up. *Freakin' MooMoo.* Just the sound of her voice made me sick.

Several days later, and with Sara's christening well planned out, I called again to fill Teddy in on the details.

"Heylowwww!" she sang.

"May I speak with Teddy please?" I asked.

"Teddy is on ice!" The MooMoo spoke proudly.

CLICK!

The bitch hung up. Not even a minute later my grandmother's phone rang. With Sara sleeping, I was able to run down to answer it.

"Hello," I picked up.

"Lem'me ahx (ask) you sum'tin… you have you baby right?" MooMoo asked in her husky French accent. I didn't say a word. I simply held the phone to see where she was going with her question.

"Isn't that what you wanted? So why don't you stop callin' haye (here) lookin' for heem (him)? If he wants to see you he will come, but obviously he doesn't care about you and you child, so get a life."

CLICK!

She hung up. I called her back, but from my line. Little did I know, the MooMoo had caller ID.

"What do you want Nishelle Maron? He doesn't want you and your bastard baby!"

CLICK!

She hung up again. She was the type of person who'd say or do her shit and run. A straight up punk - that's what she was. I called her back.

"Wh-a-a-a-at?" she answered.

"Obviously, you don't know the meaning of the word bastard and in case you haven't noticed, both of your children are bastards. Educate yourself before you start talking shit," I told her.

"You child is a bastard, just like she MUDDUH. You fahduh (father) did not raise YOU and neither will you child be raised by hers," she spoke as if she knew her words had weight.

"Oh NO?" I howled. "That's what you think bitch!"

"You watch and see - over my dead body! NISHI I HOPE YOU BASTARD BABY DIES!" she shouted.

CLICK!

She hung up. This girl was crazy. I sat down and took a deep breath.

"SATURDAY'S"

STRESSED LIKE HELL ON A SATURDAY NIGHT

NOWHERE TO GO `CAUSE MY MONEY IS TIGHT

GOT A CHILD TO CLOTHE AND OUR MOUTHS TO

BE FED

HER DADDY DIDN'T SAY WITH THIS RING I THEE

WED

TONIGHT I'M DOWN BUT TOMORROW'S ON ITS

WAY

HOPEFULLY, MY LUCK WILL CHANGE BEFORE

NEXT SATURDAY

I tried, but I just couldn't shake the anger, so that night we paid Meryl a visit.

"Yo Nish, how we gonna get in the building?" Sandra asked.

"Oh please, that's easy. When somebody comes out, I'll catch the door," I explained.

"There's somebody coming out now!" my mother pointed out.

I quickly jumped out of the van and ran up those steps in two's.

"Thanks!" I said to the tenant as he held the door open for me. Their building was equipped with the buzzer system. You ring and they buzz you in. We didn't want this, because we wanted to catch that big mouth bitch off guard. My mother and Sandra calmly walked up and entered the building behind me.

"What floor are they on?" my mother asked.

"Third," Sandra and I answered simultaneously.

"Let's take the elevator," my mother suggested.

"Nah 'cause the elevator might stop and what if one of them is waitin' to get on. Then what?" Sandra reasoned.

"If it's her, we f^@% her up and leave," my gangster mother shrugged.

"Nah - let's just take the stairs Gladys." Sandra was the first to mount the staircase.

I followed and my mother was just steps behind me.

"Nish, where's your moms?" Sandra turned and whispered, with only two steps to go just before touching down on the third floor.

"She was right behind me," I answered.

Moments later, my mother turned the corner, but still on the second floor level.

"What happened Gladys? You run out of breath?" Sandra laughed.

"I dropped my ice pick and had to go back to get it," my mother answered.

Together we approached Teddy's apartment door.

KNOCK! KNOCK! KNOCK!

Sandra rapped on the door while my mother and I stood to the sides.

"Who is it?" someone asked.

"Yo Nish, Teddy's home."

Sandra cocked her mouth to the side and stated. We didn't think that he was there; we hadn't seen his van parked outside.

"Somebody's lookin' through the peep hole," Sandra informed as she backed up. Slowly the door opened.

"What's up?" Teddy opened the door of their apartment.

"Yeah, what's up? Did you come to deliver a message for you friend?"

MooMoo asked Sandra as she stood behind Teddy looking over his shoulder. I jumped out from against the wall.

"No, I bring them myself and what did you say about my baby BITCH?" I swung at her over Teddy's shoulder. She quickly turned and ran towards the back of her apartment.

"Marlene, come!" MooMoo called her sister.

"YEAH MARLENE COME FOR YOUR ASS KICKIN' TOO!" I screamed into their apartment.

"Nishi what's going on?" Teddy asked.

"I'll tell you what's going on. Your girlfriend here called the house and told Nishi that she hopes that your daughter dies!" My mother took control of the situation.

Teddy frowned and called Meryl back to the front door.

"What's you problem gyul?" he scolded her.

"I can say what I want and if she doesn't like it, then too bad," MooMoo said with that freakin' smug look of hers. Ugly bitch!

"BITCH! COME OUT HERE AND SAY THAT SHIT. I WILL WIRE YOUR F^@%KIN' JAW!" I shouted.

"Nishi calm down," Teddy said.

"Calm down for what? Every time I turn around this bitch is either calling the house or stalking you on my block," I yelled.

"Teddy, Nishi simply called to tell you about Sara's christening and this crazy bitch starts her shit," my mother stated.

"Meryl how can you say sum'tin like that when you just had a baby you self?" Teddy continued to scold MooMoo.

"Enough of this..come inside Teddy!" Meryl tugged at his shirt.

Teddy ignored her command and continued to talk to my mother.

"Teddy you need to be a man and stand up to this girl. I mean come on... just a couple of weeks ago you met me at the subway station, crying your eyes out about how much you love Nishi," my mother revealed while everyone else stood in silence.

"COME INSIDE I SAID!" Meryl shouted and pulled on Teddy's shirt again.

It wasn't long before Teddy grew tired of being jerked around. After that last pull, he brushed her off and stepped further out into the hallway.

"CALL DEE COPS MARLENE!" Meryl shouted.

"Call dee cops for what? Cause I'm talkin' to me child's mudduh?" Teddy cut his eye at Meryl.

"You are MY man! You are MY husband, so why in the hell are you talkin' to this slut and she mudduh? All I have to say is like mudduh.. like dottuh." This baboon would not stop. Her mouth was going to get her killed.

"See what I'm talking about. You need to put her disrespectful ass in her place," my mother told Teddy as she slid slowly towards their apartment doorway. My mother was sneaky and knowing her, she was moving in for the kill.

"Meryl why don't you come outside and play!" Sandra smiled. We were itching to kick her ass.

"Someone up here called for the police?" A male voice came from the other end of the hallway. Everyone turned to look.

"Yes, I did," Meryl came out of the apartment.

"Who are you?" The approaching officer asked.

"I am HIS wife!" Meryl said firmly while pointing to Teddy.

"Can you come inside because I don't want to talk to you in frunt'tuh dem (front of them)?" She glanced at us and jerked her head upward.

"Boy-y-y!" I clenched my teeth.

"Follow us sir!" the officer told Teddy.

"While my partner's inside getting their side of the story, you three can tell me yours," the second officer said to me and my partners in crime. We explained to the officer that Meryl's phone call to the house was rather disturbing and how we simply came to talk to her about it. He laughed and shook his head in disbelief. He knew good and well we weren't there to talk.

While outside laughing with the other officer, the lead policeman exited the apartment and approached us.

"Alright, here's the deal. Who's the girlfriend out here?" He asked.

"I am," I spoke up.

"How old are you?"

"Twenty one."

"I'm tellin' you right now, you need to leave this man alone. Do you know she has a newborn baby inside?"

"Yeah, I know. And my baby's two days older than hers."

"Wait a minute! You have a baby with this guy too?" the officer asked in amazement.

"Yeah, that's the reason we're here. She called my house earlier talking shit and told me that she hopes my baby dies," I explained.

"Like I said, you need to leave this guy alone. He's sittin' in there like he's scared to talk. He looks pretty confused and this girl that he's living with - why did he have a baby with her?" he laughed. New York's Finest evidently found Meryl to be a MooMoo as well.

"So what's this about him being her husband?" I raised a new argument.

"I don't know HOT HEAD but when I asked him if they were married, HE said no. She was probably just sayin' that to get you upset and look at you... you fell for it. Seriously though, you need to get out of this relationship 'cause somebody's either gonna get hurt or arrested. You're a good lookin' girl and I'm sure you can find somebody else out there with less drama 'cause this guy has some serious issues."

The lead officer broke it down to me.

"No doubt! No doubt!" Sandra agreed.

"Now that everyone's all nice and calm, let's all go home and relax 'cause I know you's really didn't come here to talk." These cops were straight up Italians. You could hear the ricotta cheese in their dialect.

One by one we descended the staircase with the officers at the front of the line.

"Where's the other one?" The second officer asked after suddenly turning around.

My mother was no longer behind us. Immediately, both officers turned and took off back upstairs. Sandra and I remained on the staircase oblivious to this entire situation.

"Where's your moms Nish?" Sandra whispered.

"I don't know!" I shrugged my shoulders.

She and I stood on that staircase fully unaware that my mother had slipped us. *This isn't looking good.*

"Where were you?" We heard one of the officers ask.

"I was looking for my watch. It must have fallen off while we were upstairs," my mother answered as we finally made it to the bottom.

"Alright ladies, you have a good night," the officers said as they watched us enter the van.

"Gladys what happened? Why did you go back upstairs?" Sandra asked as I pulled off.

"I forgot my ice pick. When the cops got there, I stashed it behind the staircase just in case they wanted to search somebody." At times, I found my mother's behavior to be a little strange, but at least, she was always a step ahead.

———————————

Several months went by with Teddy and I struggling to hold on to what we had. Seeing his daughter every other month was not my idea of being a father and life with my daughter was becoming a challenge. I was now the only one buying pampers and formula. Luckily for me, Renee' filled me in on the Public Assistance application process and how it worked. Had it not been for her, I would have been totally screwed.

One hot August morning I went down to sterilize and prepare Sara's bottles while she slept.

"BOO!" My mother emerged from the basement.

"What are you doing home?" I asked.

"I didn't feel like going in today, so... Nish I got a surprise for you," she said with this huge grin on her face.

"What is it?" An image suddenly appeared from behind her.

"What happened? Did you escape?" I asked him.

They both laughed, but I was dead serious. My mother hadn't mentioned that Ethon was coming out. Come to think of it, I do remember her taking several milk like baths last winter. She claimed that her "spiritual" baths would make him come live with her upon his release date.

Every night for about a week, she'd fill the tub with HOT water, add a creamy white liquid along with some type of flowers or petals then would submerge her entire body in the solution. As she relaxed in this *come live with me* potion, in her hand she held the Holy Bible and would flip through the testaments.

She had become infatuated with this *"spiritual"* mess. During her evening ritual, no one was allowed to enter the bathroom because she'd always lock the door. Again, her weird behavior led me to question her character. According to her, a spiritual adviser instructed her to perform this daily practice to obtain the partner that she so very much desired.

"He got out today," my mother said.

Today? It was only 9:00 A.M. Damn! Alert us civilians before releasing the felonious folk.

"Why were you in the basement?" I then asked her.

"'Cause I'm movin' into the basement. I need a bigger place for me and my family."

"Oh okay. Well, I'll leave you two to your moving. Thank God your belongings are only two flights away," I joked.

For the first time ever, my thirty-six year old mother had just moved out of her upstairs sleeping quarters and into her mother's basement apartment. So HE'S the reason for this reconstruction.

Months ago, Grams had arranged for her basement to be converted into a semi apartment, two bedrooms and a living room. Unfortunately, the construction was never completed, which made it mandatory that the tenants use our upstairs bathroom.

This was cumbersome at times because it was the only working facility throughout the three level house. For years, Grams had been asking El Creepo to fix the bathroom on the first floor, but Mr. Shuffle didn't move fast enough, so it remained unusable.

After work, his lazy ass would entertain himself with his collection of Mighty Morphan Power Rangers and happy meal toys from McDonald's. Smoking a joint or two would cause the already zoned out one to remain beamed into that other dimension for a little while longer. This guy even had the nerve to label his belongings and dared anyone to touch them.

WOOF! WOOF! WOOF! WOOF! WOOF!

My Rottweiler buddy appeared.

"Oh shoots!" Ethon cried out and backed away from the dog.

"MOVE KYRA!" I shouted at her. Kyra was a very playful dog and had never jumped at any one like that before. It was weird.

"Nishi why is your beast trying to eat up my man?" my mother sighed.

"Time for me to go! My baby's bottle is warm enough and she's probably up by now. Come on Kyra." I tugged on my 100 lbs. friend's collar.

Later that afternoon, Ethon approached me about my motorcycle.

"Yo Nish, can I get a ride off your bike?" he asked.

"How are you gonna ride and you just got out of prison?" I responded.

"Who's gonna know? Come on. Stop being such a chicken, you know I didn't raise you like that."

I grew guilty; after all he was the one who taught me how to drive a stick and threw me his keys daring me to take a ride on his motorcycle when I was just a young kid. I owed him one.

"Alright, I'mma get my key, but only a quick ride around the block Ethon."

By the time I returned, Ethon was already in the backyard and had unlocked the back gate.

"Where's Kyra?" I nervously looked around.

"I don't know," he answered.

"KYRA-A-A-A!" I screamed.

Two seconds later, I saw her shadow coming down the driveway. Luckily, the front gate wasn't opened or she would have been gone.

"I didn't even realize that she got out," Ethon said, apologetically.

"Here's the key. ONLY around the block," I looked him straight in the eye.

"Nishi, I know you didn't let that man ride your motorcycle without a license," Grams stated while placing her belongings on the kitchen table after a long day at work. Obviously, she had seen the deal go down.

"He only went around the block," I answered.

"And what if he did?" my mother asked in an impudent tone while ascending the basement stairs.

"I wasn't talking to you Gladys... I was talking to Nishi," Grams snapped as she turned to face her daughter. "And what if something happens while his ass is out there on it?"

"Then I'll just buy her another one," my mother mindlessly shrugged. *Please who are you foolin'? I do*

remember Sandra tellin' you, **"Gladys I could lend you the**
money and you could pay me back when you get it."
Always trying to act like money is not an issue.

VROOM! VROOM! Ethon revved the bike as he
pulled into the garage.

Grams looked up at me and shook her head in
disgust. "Y'all sure do some crazy shit!"

"Here Nish, tanks (thanks). Oh hi Moms," Ethon
greeted Grams as he handed me my keys.

"Mmmm hmmm," Grams nodded and walked
away...

The next day he was back there washing my
motorcycle as if it were his pride and joy. *What in the*
world is this guy's problem? With another man in the house
now, El Creepo kept a low profile. He no longer slept nor

played in the living room like before. Things changed a bit, but was it for the better?

RING!

My phone rang. I hit the speaker button.

"Hello?" I answered.

"Nish!" Renee' said.

"Yeah, what's up?" I asked.

"You got me on speaker phone?" she asked.

"Yeah, why?"

"Take me off!" Renee' instructed. From the tone in her voice I could tell that something was wrong.

"Alright, hold up cause I'm changing Sara's pamper."

After adhering the second strap to the front of Sara's pamper, I took hold of the receiver.

"Okay, what's up Ree?"

"I just got off the phone with your mother and do you know she told me she no longer needs me to work for her."

"Why not?" I asked, shaking my head. "School's starting back next week."

"I know... that's why I called her but right before I called her, I was telling Paul Gladys should be calling me soon with the schedule for the new school year. He then suggested that I call her instead of waiting on her to call me... anyway, when I asked her 'why not?' she told me that Ethon was going to do it."

"You're lying," I said in amazement.

"No I'm not. That shit is SO f^@%'d up," she whispered. "When was she gonna tell me? And to make matters worse, I was depending on that extra money this year."

"Renee' I don't know what to tell you."

"Anyway, I just called to tell you how f^@%'d up your mother is. I'll talk to you later." My cousin hung up.

I could tell that she was crying. Like myself, she was having a hard time too. She needed every dollar that she could get. Especially since she was trying to move out of her basement apartment that would occasionally become flooded after rainy days.

––––––––––––––––

"Where's Kyra?" I asked Grams one weekend afternoon while placing Sara in her walker.

"I don't know."

"MOMMY!" I yelled.

"Yeah." she yelled back.

"Is Kyra down there?"

"No. Why would she be down here?"

"I'm just asking `cause she's not up here nor is she in the backyard."

I quickly ran upstairs to put on some street clothes.

"Grams watch Sara for me while I go and look for Kyra." I hurried through the back door. This was the second time now that my dog had gone missing.

Just as I reached the front gate, two familiar looking teenagers approached the house.

"Miss is this your dog?" One teen asked as the other held onto Kyra's collar.

"Yeah," I frowned at them both. I was happy and shocked with this outcome.

"We saw her down the block. She was just standing there and I remembered seeing her in your front yard one day, that's how I knew to bring her back here."

"Thank you! I really appreciate it," I said and grabbed hold of Kyra's collar.

"She's a pretty dog. You shouldn't let her get out like that," the teen then added.

I thanked him again, but deep down inside I was livid. *Damn dog, you allowed someone to touch you. What kind of attack dog are you?* I opened the back gate and ordered her to go in. "Get your ass in there!"

As we approached the back door, Grams was there looking out for us. Immediately, she opened the door and quickly, Kyra ran inside.

"Where did you find her Nishi?" Grams asked.

"Two teenager boys brought her back."

"Teenagers? From where?"

"They said she was just standing there. The idiot most likely didn't know which way home was," I stated while filling a bucket of water to bathe her. Kyra's coat seemed a bit dusty and she smelled like hell.

"That's a damn shame," Grams shook her head. "Why is she getting' out so often? This never happened until Ethon came here and I realize too that he keeps movin' the wooden stick I laid across the basement doorway. I already told him to stop movin' it because I put it there to prevent Sara from falling down those steps and he'll move it every damn time. I bet you he's the one that let Kyra out too," she argued.

"I KNOW he's the one because every time he opens the back gate, she runs out," I said, fully supporting Grams's theory. Ethon was starting to get on my nerves. He had no respect for other people's belongings.

My speculation was confirmed the day he modified the appearance of the van. I couldn't believe what he had done to my work of art.

On the right rear quarter panel of the van was a massive dent. *And what's that sweet burning smell?* I inspected the interior of my old work station. Ethon found his accident to be somewhat hilarious, but then again, almost everything was a joke to him. Grams and I both found his asinine behavior to be extremely annoying.

"MOMMY!"

"YEAH!"

"Can you come up here for a minute please?"

"What do you want?" She rudely asked while standing just a few steps shy from the top of the basement stairs.

"Do me a favor and tell Ethon to close the gate behind him when he's leaving. This is the second time now that Kyra's gotten out," I explained. Grams looked on without saying a word.

"Why does it have to be Ethon that's letting her out?" my mother asked defensively.

"Because Mommy, even up to this moment, I just went out into the backyard and the gate was ajar. Ethon's the only one so far who left through the back gate today. Didn't he pull the van out earlier?"

"AND?" she once again defensively asked.

"AND ANOTHER THING… that van is still in my name and he's drivin' it all over the damn place. When are you going to take that van out of my name, huh?" Grams asked, taking over the conversation.

"As soon as I'm finish making my payments on it."

"Well I hope that's soon because the dealer called here the other day too. They haven't received this month's payment yet," Grams informed my mother.

"I mailed it yesterday," my mother replied.

"YESTERDAY? They're supposed to have it by now. You're screwing up my credit Gladys."

"Is this what y'all called me up here for?"

"We just wanted to talk to you about Ethon because he seems to do whatever he wants and that ain't gonna make it around here!" Grams told her.

"Funny how you didn't feel that way when El Creepo moved in and tried to run things," my mother smugly stated. The intensity of the conversation magnified. I just wanted her to talk to her man, but from her responses, I sensed that she felt as if we were condemning Ethon.

"THIS IS MY F^@%KIN' HOUSE AND I CAN HAVE WHO I WANNA HAVE IN HERE. NOW IF YOU DON'T LIKE IT YOU AND YOUR MAN CAN FIND SOMEWHERE ELSE TO LIVE!" Grams shouted to the top of her lungs. My mother didn't say a word after that; she just rolled her eyes and returned to the pit...

Three months later, Kyra had eleven puppies. My intuition told me she was pregnant because before she went missing, she was experiencing her first estrus cycle, (the stage of the reproductive cycle in which the dog can become pregnant.) Yet, days after the teens returned her, I realized that her cycle was gone. Plus, her weight gain was another hunch.

Unfortunately, Kyra did not demonstrate that maternal instinct that a mother should, so I had to intervene while she delivered her young. As soon as her puppies entered the world, she abandoned them. Instead of caring for them, she ran and dragged the first set of puppies around by its umbilical cord while the placenta remained inside her vagina. Eventually, it plopped out, enabling room for the next pup to exit through the birth canal, but her actions caused me to grow worrisome.

"NO KYRA - LAY DOWN! LAY DOWN!" It didn't work.

She stood watching strangely as her newborns wiggled their way out of their sac. This was wrong and scary, so I ran inside and called the veterinarian.

Within moments, I returned to the garage wearing a pair of surgical gloves to eliminate the human scent which could cause the animal to kill and eat its pups. From the house, Dr. Nishelle Maron also collected a pair of scissors, some thread and a roll of paper towel to wipe away the excess blood - I became that veterinarian after all.

I tied the thread around the puppies' belly then cut the cord. Normally, the mother would remove the sac, chew off the umbilical cord and then eat the afterbirth. This was not the case. A human's interference could be risky, but Kyra was so confused and in pain to the point where she just simply watched on. After caring for the fourth pup or so, the domesticated beast began to show signs of interest. She slowly approached her offspring and began to lick them. This was her way of telling me to back off. I watched from a distance and in time, all of nature's once needed parts were devoured by the bitch. Several hours later her mutts were already trying to stand up...

Winter was here again and apparently, Teddy defrosted himself because he unexpectedly stopped by one day.

"So I see that you're no longer on ice," I said after opening the front door.

"What? What are you talking about?" he frowned.

"The last time I called your house, which was MONTHS ago, you were on ice," I stressed, kindly letting him know that his lengthy absence was unacceptable. Like Simon, his *simple* ass took a seat on the floor in the corner of my room while cuddling *he dottuh.*

"What is that supposed to mean'?" Slowly he looked up at me.

"I don't know. Ask your bitch!"

"Nishi I didn't come haye for this shit. I hear dee same shit from she," he said, rolling his eyes.

"Well buddy, it sounds to me that you have a personal problem," I showed no remorse. *My daughter and I haven't seen you in months and you think that I should feel sorry for you? Bullshit! I will no longer be your foolish puppet.*

"Oh and in case you didn't know, your daughter's birthday was months ago," I bitterly stated.

"You tink me don't know dat? Why you tink me haye now?"

"NOW?" I snapped. "Man-n-n, what part didn't you understand? I said MONTHS AGO. It's now what – the end of FEBRUARY? You DIDN'T attend her party, but I bet your ass was present for your son's first birthday though. Also, she took her first step on the day before her birthday, but you're probably not too interested in her physical progression either."

"Why do you have to say sum'tin like dat?" he asked.

"Because it's true!" I screamed. "Actions speak louder than words. You don't call or anything. So what would you like for me to say to you? Hello sweetie - how was your vacation? ASS WIPE!"

His eyes flooded with tears.

"Don't start your bitch ass cryin' up in here!" I scolded him. "Every time you do somethin' stupid, you come running back to me hoping that I'll sympathize with your simple ass. But NOT this time!"

"But Nishi, you don't understand how I feel. You don't have to talk to me like that!"

"How YOU feel? F^@% HOW YOU FEEL!" I yelled. "Have you ever taken a moment to even think about how I feel when I don't hear or see you for months at a time? You just totally stopped buying pampers and milk. I mean, how do you expect for me to talk to you?"

"She need pampers now?"

His dense question led me to believe that his brain still had some thawing out to do.

"She's gonna always need pampers until she's potty trained. Or maybe I should just let her shit in your mouth 'cause right now that's all you're talkin'. Shit!"

I verbally abused him. If words could hurt, he would have had many welts.

"She sit'tin on she potty chay (chair) yet?"

"Sometimes," I answered reluctantly.

For a good thirty minutes or so, we sat silently in my room admiring our daughter.

"So do you care to tell me why we haven't seen you for so long?" I broke the silence.

"Nishi. Just forget about it. I'm haye now, right?"

"Yeah and after you leave here today, we won't see you for another year right? Asshole." I whispered the Asshole part.

"Nishi. I love you, but right now its ha'ad (hard) for me."

"LOVE ME? HARD FOR YOU? How do you think I feel? I KNOW it ain't love that brought you here today. WHAT? You want some pussy? What's wrong she ain't givin' up hers and so you thought that old faithful Nishi would spread 'em wide and pour out all of her love for you huh? Well you know what?"

I reached for my telephone receiver. "I'm gonna show you just how much I am tired of your ass, 'cause I can do bad on my own."

I proceeded to dial a number on the keypad.

"Heylo?" MooMoo answered her phone.

"Your man is here. Why don't you come and get him?" I told her.

"I knew that he was going out to see you!" she angrily responded.

Meanwhile Teddy sat quietly with Sara in his arms. Probably was thinking to himself, *I need a drink and a joint*!

"You tell him that I said to stay there because as of now he is no longer my husband."

CLICK! She hung up.

"Why does this bitch keep calling you her husband?" I asked him as I placed the receiver on its base.

"I don't know."

"What do you mean you don't know? Is there something you need to tell me?"

"No!" Teddy frowned.

"Are you married?" I rephrased the questioned.

"What did I tell you? No right! That's she shit. Before I left dee house she tell me dat if she finds out dat I came haye to see you and dee baby then she was goin' to do sum'tin crazy."

"Like what?" I asked, rolling my eyes.

"And I belĭv (believe) she too 'cause you see dee fuss (first) time when she found out about us she did sum'tin dat made me belĭv dat she'd do it."

"Like what?" I asked.

"She took me son to dee kitchen window and tret'ten to tro' he (threatened to throw him) out."

"You're lying," I shook my head in disbelief.

"No... and at dee time he was only a few munts (months) old."

"Did you call the police?"

"No, because I tell she dat I would stop talkin' to you. I just wanted she to put dee boy down."

"Okay, so are you telling me she's threatening you through your sons'?"

"Yeah, dat's dee only reason why me still daye (there). I don't love she. I love you and she knows dat. She rip me jacket tryin' to kip (keep) me from lĭvin (leaving) dee house. She said dat she knew dat I was comin' to see me two bitches."

"Bitches! What two bitches?"

"You and Sara. She said instead of one whore I now have two to visit."

"And what did you say?"

"I just tell she to shut she ass up and me leave dee house."

"So MooMoo's making you stay away from your daughter by threatening to kill your sons? She needs a serious ass kickin'," I grew annoyed.

"Dis isn't dee fuss (first) time that me and she had it out like dis - we fought befo' (before)." Teddy revealed.

"And?" I waited for the punch line.

"And she call dee cops on me. They say dat if they had to come back to dee apa'tment (apartment) then boat'a we (both of us) get'ten arrested."

"You have a problem on your hands," I stated.

"Look, take dee baby. I'm livin' (leaving) before she does sum'tin else stchu'pid (stupid)."

Teddy stood up.

"And here's sixty dollars for you to buy pampers and whatever else the baby needs."

Teddy handed me a fifty and a ten dollar bill.

"Wait! Gimme back dee ten!" Teddy ordered.

"What? For what?" I frowned.

"Cause I wanna buy a bag of weed."

I couldn't believe this pot head. I didn't say a word. I calmly handed him back the ten dollar bill and followed him to the front door.

Carefully we stepped around Kyra's ten healthy and playful puppies as they crowded our feet in the vestibule. Unfortunately, one, the runt, didn't make it.

"Shi-i-i-t muhn when did she have all these puppies?" Teddy asked.

"While you were on ice!" I snickered.

He looked at me as if I had said something wrong. Hell. I was simply answering his question with the information that I was given.

"Good-bye Nishi!"

"Whatever!" I shut the door.

Although Sara was walking well enough on her own now, I'd sometimes put her in the walker to keep her from getting into things as I prepared her meals and/or fed Kyra's puppies. Unfortunately, Kyra never adapted to the whole motherhood thing and trying to get her to nurse those puppies was a bit of a task.

In a way, I couldn't blame her though, those puppies of hers were fierce. They literally ran down their lactating mother for food. Every day she would try to out run them, but eventually, she'd grow tired and lay down. Only to tolerate a few minutes of constant clawing and sucking on her red blotchy nipples that seemed to be very sore. There were times when she absolutely refused to be in the same room with them. I then had to take the feeding process to the next level which was feeding them from a bottle. That puppy milk was expensive and I was delighted when they turned three months old; puppy chow was now on their menu.

Plus, they were now at the age that I could pass them over to the North Shore Animal League out in Long Island, New York. There I knew they'd be properly cared for until a loving family would adopt them. Turning them over wasn't as easy as I thought it would be though. An examination was required prior to the acceptance of any animal and because I had ten of those jokers, it took me some time to get an appointment for all of them on the same day.

But before I could make that trip out to Long Island with them, I heard a loud thump one afternoon.

Immediately, I left the puppies alone and ran like hell towards the kitchen. Sara was screaming at the top of her lungs. Grams was just approaching the basement door when I flew pass her and down those stairs. At the bottom stood Ethon with Sara in his arms. He had already removed her from the overturned walker and was trying to comfort her.

"Gimme my baby!" I screamed. Ethon obeyed my order.

I performed a quick check of her from head to toe. She appeared to be fine. There weren't any bruises or bumps but she was crying hysterically. I held my shaken baby close to my chest as I hastily ascended those 15 stairs.

"WHO IN THE F^@% MOVED THIS STICK THAT I LAID HERE ACROSS THIS DOORWAY?" Grams yelled as I sat at the kitchen table thoroughly examining her great granddaughter that shared the same zodiac sign. The two were born in the month of October but only a day apart. Sara's birthday was on the 15th and Grams's birthday was on the 16th.

"I TOLD Y'ALL NOT TO MOVE IT AND YET YOU STILL TOUCHED THE DAMN THING. I WANNA KNOW WHO MOVED IT AND STOOD IT UP AGAINST THIS WALL HERE?" Grams was livid.

Not a peep from the pit. Ethon nor my mother said a word. I mean it was absolute stillness. It was as if no one was even down there. The basements are usually colder than the other parts of the house. Could the "Black Mamba" and her "Salipenter" have gone into hibernation already?

Grams took a seat next to me, also examining my very agitated daughter, who had finally stopped crying at least.

"You okay baby?" She rubbed Sara's head and face.

"Nishi even though she looks fine, I think that you should still take her to the hospital," Grams suggested. "That baby fell down a full flight of steps and those steps are hard."

"For what? She's not bleeding and I don't see any bruises. Why should I go and sit up in Kings County for six hours when the only thing they're gonna do is examine her, just as we already did, and tell me to just keep an eye on her in case her behavior changes."

Grams was only trying to help, but I was still very upset about the situation.

"I know Nishi, but maybe they will see something we didn't."

"Grams, if she acts any differently or starts crying again, then I'll take her. But until then, I'm not going anywhere." During our brief conversation, the serpents never came upstairs to apologize for moving that stick...

Several weeks after Sara's mishap, Kyra somehow managed to get out of the backyard again – but this time she never came back. I was pissed, but what could I do? Sara was now my biggest responsibility and things were starting to pick up. I was now working for an insurance agency on Wall Street in Manhattan as a temporary employee and I was about to become permanent.

"Nish - what's wrong with Sara's eye?" Evelyn stopped by to pay us a visit one evening.

She was focusing something serious on Sara's right eye.

"What's wrong with her eye?" I reciprocated her question.

"She has this hazy look in it," Evelyn stated. Of course, I got up to take a look and sure enough, something was there.

"I don't know what it is, but I'll be sure to ask the doctor about it. She's scheduled for a routine visit next week, so I'll find out then," I explained.

For a while we sat in silence, knowing that whatever was in her eye was serious. Just when my life seemed to shine again, the unknown appeared to weaken that glare. Something was always going on. Every now and then, Grams and I would hear the serpents hissing at one another. Ethon would come and go at wee hours in the morning with the van. Every week the van had a new scratch and Lee was now calling him daddy. What was my mother thinking?

That following week we visited the doctor as scheduled.

"Sara Maron-Ruthbun!" We stood up, I gathered our belongings, then headed for one of the many examining rooms. Usually, they took her height and weight first, so without them having to tell me - I removed her shoes.

"Hello pretty little girl. I remember you. How are you today?" The nurse initiated some small chat. Sara wasn't the type to panic at the site of white coats. She always remained cool.

"I just wanna get your height and weight okay, so can you stand here for me please?"

My plump faced Sara walked over and mounted the scale. I must say, my daughter was adorable.

"Thank you Sara!" The nurse gave her a lollypop.

"The doctor should be with you momentarily, okay Mrs. Ruthbun?" She said while slightly pulling the door shut. *Mrs. Ruthbun? I wish.*

Moments later the doctor entered the room.

"Hello! Haven't seen you two in a while - how are we doing today?" The doctor rubbed Sara's head.

"We're fine," I answered.

"Okay - let's see here. What are we doing today?" He looked at her chart. "Little Sara you'll be getting only one injection today - aren't you the lucky one!" he smiled.

"Doctor there's something that I would like for you to take a look at but I'll wait until after she receives her immunization," I informed him.

"No. Please show me now. After the injection she may not want me to touch her."

I pointed to Sara's right eye.

"My aunt noticed a grayish image covering her pupil." I stated and backed away allowing the physician to examine her eye completely.

"Okay, little lady open wide for me." He combed her eyes with the Ophthalmoscope.

"Yeah - your aunt's right. There's no question that she has something wrong with her right eye. When did you first notice this?" he asked.

"About a week ago. My aunt was holding her and realized that she had this hazy appearance in it."

"Were there any problems at birth?" he asked me.

"No.

"She was full term right?"

"Yes, but about a month ago she fell down a flight of steps as she moved throughout the house in her walker. There weren't any obvious bruises so I didn't take her to the emergency room."

"She had no bruises?" the pediatrician asked in amazement.

"No. Not one. Not even a scratch," I answered.

"I never did like those walkers and for that very same reason - the fear of a child falling down a staircase. It seems to me that she may have a cataract and the fall most likely could have caused it."

My heart dropped and my conscious grew guilty.

"I have a question," I stated.

"Sure. What is it?"

"If I would have taken her to the emergency room directly after the fall, would they have noticed this then?"

"No. If the patient isn't bleeding, has no swelling or showing any signs of struggling, then no they wouldn't have. A cataract develops as time progresses. It's an optical aging disease, usually common in the elderly. I would like for another one of our doctors to take a look at it to get a second opinion. Can you give me one moment and I'll be right back?

"Sure." The doctor then exited the room. *I can't believe this shit. This jailbird asshole has caused more damage than I thought.* I took Sara in my arms and held her tightly.

KNOCK! KNOCK!

Both doctors' entered the room. The second pediatrician entered first.

"Hello. I would like to take a look at your daughter's eye. I understand that she wasn't born like this but recently fell down a flight of stairs in a walker?" The second pediatrician gathered some facts.

"Yes, that's correct," I answered.

"Again, when did she fall?" he asked, while scrutinizing my daughter's right eye with his mini flashlight.

"About a month ago."

"Yeah, this is definitely a cataract caused by trauma," he assured us.

Again my heart dropped. *My poor baby!* I began to blame myself. *If I hadn't been feeding those damn puppies then I could have stopped her from approaching that unsafe doorway.* Tears began to flood my eyes.

"She'll be fine Ms. Ruthbun. But, for sure she's going to need surgery in order to correct the vision in that eye. I'll have the nurse write up a referral for you. I would like for her to be seen by the Ophthalmologist right across the hall. Over there, he'll be able to explain to you in depth exactly what's going on with your daughter's eye and how they would like to proceed, but I'm pretty sure it's a cataract."

To expedite the referral process, the doctor prepared the paperwork himself. Both professionals wished me luck then moved on to their next patient.

Curious to know if there was an alternative method for us out there, I got a second opinion from the doctors at the N.Y. Eye and Ear Infirmary in Manhattan. They had the same solution – SURGERY. By the end of May, Sara was scheduled for surgery, but unfortunately, she caught the Chicken Pox from another child at the babysitter's house. I informed the doctor and her surgery was postponed...

Months later, one very brisk fall morning, Sara and I entered the Ambulatory Surgery Department at Long Island College Hospital to begin the admitting process. Registration was easy, but the thought of my baby going under had my stomach bubbling.

At exactly 7:00 a.m., the nurses' prepared my innocent daughter for the rigorous procedure. After inserting her I.V. and connecting the monitors, the anesthesiologist administered a gel like suppository, which sedated her. Some thirty minutes later, the head nurse rolled her out of the prep area on the infant crib that she had fallen asleep in. I took a deep breath and asked God to watch over my unsullied little girl; she was now in His hands.

Alone and petrified, I paced those corridors. I had to endure this frightening ordeal alone. Teddy nor my mother was present. My mother claimed that she hadn't accrued any "personal" time since joining the post office and Teddy, his excuse was pretty much the same. He had just started a new job too. A real job! One with benefits. This was the time that I needed them the most. Instead, they elected to work rather than to support their love ones.

As I strolled different sections of the hospital, something told me to look up. To my surprise, Evelyn was rushing towards me.

"Hey, I'm on my lunch hour now. I hopped on the bus and ran like three blocks to get here. How's she doin'?" Evelyn panted.

"She's okay. One of the nurses came out a while ago and asked me if I was the mother of the two year old that was having the eye surgery. I answered yes and immediately after, I asked her if something was wrong. She said 'no'. She just wanted to inform me that the procedure was going as planned and not to worry," I explained to my aunt.

"How long has she been in the operating room?" Evelyn asked.

"About three hours now."

"Well don't worry. Like the nurse said, she'll be alright. I just came to see how she was doin'. Let me head back. I have twenty minutes left, so I better get a move on and if she's as tough as her mommy, she'll pull through this just fine. Call me later and let me know how things went."

"Okay," I responded, then she and I walked in the opposite direction...

"Ms. Maron!" That same nurse called out to me as soon as I re-entered the waiting room.

"Yes?"

"Sara's in the recovery room now. Follow me please!" The nurse turned to walk.

"How is she?" I asked as we hastily walked through the hall.

"Despite the fact that she's fighting off the doctors' and crying for you, I'd say that she's doin' extremely well. Sara's a strong little girl and I have to tell you when you see your daughter, her eye is going to be covered with bandages and you may see some blood."

"Is her eye still bleeding?" I grew nervous.

"No, it's only coagulated blood, but I have to inform you because some parents become alarmed and start to freak out when they see it," she explained.

"I'll be alright," I assured the nurse.

"I'm sure you will. You seem like it and weren't you the one that was inquiring about an observation room?"

"Yeah, it was me! I wanted to be there for everything - when they put her under and brought her to, but unfortunately, this hospital doesn't allow it and so I had to be there with her in spirit."

"You're good! I don't think that I'd be able to witness my child undergo something like that," the nurse earnestly stated. Upon entering the large recovery room, I took a deep breath.

"Okay Ms. Maron, your daughter's over there in bed number two and if you need me just press the red call button on the wall."

Within proximity of her bedside railing, she turned and looked at me.

"Mommy!" she cried and reached out. I quickly took her in my arms and held her like never before.

Over the next several months, we attended therapy two, sometimes three times a week. It was a lot of work. Hoping like hell that someday I'd do away with public assistance, I managed to work as a temp here and there. Well, at least right up until welfare informed me during a re-certification appointment that they were going to deduct ten percent of my cash allowances for six months because an employer had reported my wages.

I submitted a claim to the Department of Social Security on Sara's behalf and to my surprise, it was denied. Their reason was that my baby had to be blind in both eyes in order for her to be eligible for benefits.

Each path led me to a dead end. The system confused me. They claimed that these benefits were there to aid those in dire situations. If so, why was I getting the run around? It was all planned from day one. Just hours after the delivery of a newborn, a staff member would present the recovering mother with a set of forms for her to apply for the newborn's birth certificate and *social security card,*

According to a hospital administrator, the parents would receive the card faster if the completed forms were submitted prior to being discharged. Not even a day old yet and Uncle Sam is looking to collect. The government moves fast!

Did you really believe that they were really interested in knowing what Diamante "Junebug" Dalik and Shaquisha Markita named their child? Nine digits with a heartbeat aka GUINEA PIGS! That is what we are. Think about it! Immunizations, do we need them? Do we really know what they're injecting our children with?

From the moment you exit the doctor's office your child is running a fever or developing a rash resulting from the FOUR injections that were *supposedly* necessary for your child's day care enrollment process. Doctors are constantly informing us that vaccines and/or booster shots will allegedly prevent or lessen the chance of our offspring developing any future deadly diseases. They aren't sure themselves, which is why there are so many malpractice suits in existence. How many of you have had a doctor notify you regarding your medical condition and come to find out – your prognosis is *not quite* the case? That's why getting a second opinion is wise.

It's now raining pesticides. From helicopters they're spraying our communities with chemicals that are slowly weakening our immune system. Seems like every second, a family member or friend has developed asthma. What are we inhaling? What are we eating? What are we drinking? Even better, what are we?

An individual or a team of scientists *coincidentally* stumbles across a treatment, but rarely a cure for the existing diseases or potentially deadly plagues. What happens after that? The gluttonous human like creatures patent and market the drugs. The end result, the individuals and their families live COMFORTABLY ever after. This is my definition of clinical recycling. It's all about generating money.

YOU HAVE EXCEEDED YOUR DAILY SPENDING ALLOWANCE. This automated response really irks my nerves. If I have the money in my bank account and I want to withdraw (x) amount at the ATM and later, purchase an item for (x) amount in that same day –

then let me. They claim the action is for the account

holder's protection. Simply put - we need to educate

ourselves and not allow them to benefit from our ignorance!

"WHY THE UNNECESSARY?"

I WAS BORN BLACK, I WAS BORN BEAUTIFUL

I WAS BORN A FEMALE, I WAS BORN STRONG

I WASN'T BORN WITHOUT EMOTIONS!

Although Sara and I conquered the initial obstacle, we still had many hurdles to leap. Yes, the cataract was removed, but the therapeutic role was extremely tedious for us both. In order for her to regain strength and a percentage of her eyesight back, she wore a contact lens in the right eye and a patch covering her left eye. This daily practice was implemented to force her to utilize that right eye with the hope that it would not become lazy. The chances of her ever being able to see from that eye again was very slim, but it was worth a try. Positioning and keeping a contact lens in a two year old's eye was almost impossible. A teary eye or even a simple rub would cause the lens to shift.

Upon my arrival at the babysitter's house late one afternoon, I realized that Sara didn't have the lens on her eye. The babysitter and I combed that hardwood floor, but of course we never found it. Medicaid refused to kick out for another one, so out of my pocket came that one hundred and seventy-five dollars for a replacement. Unfortunately, some weeks later, Sara lost the second one. I cried like a baby because I was trying so hard to be a good mother while at the same time trying to make a dollar. The pressure overwhelmed me.

After overhearing me mention Sara's lost contact lenses, my mother stated that she would contribute something towards the third one; I never saw a cent and as for Teddy, he was missing in action AGAIN. Sick and tired, but still full of hope, I gave the Ophthalmologist a call. He insisted that I get another lens and soon too.

"What about eyeglasses?" I asked during our telephone conversation.

"Eyeglasses aren't as effective as the lenses. The eyeglasses sit off of the eye whereas the lenses sit directly on the eye enabling her to focus better on objects," he explained.

After terminating the call with the doctor, I gave Teddy a call to seek his assistance on Sara's situation.

"Hello?" he answered in his timid voice.

"What's with you?" I asked.

"What do you mean, 'What's wit me?'" Teddy huffed.

"That weed must be REAL strong 'cause I haven't heard from you in months. What, you forgot that you have a daughter over here?" I jeered.

"Dat's how it tiz nowadays. Me only one puh'sun (person) and I can't be in two places at one time," he boldly stated.

"Yeah, but you found time to be in two pussies at one time though – right?" I smirked.

"Gyul! What do you want?"

"Your daughter needs a new lens. She lost the first two and I can't afford to buy another one, so how much are you going to contribute?"

"How much is dee lens?" Teddy asked.

"One hundred and seventy-five dollars."

"So much for only one lens?" he complained.

"Yep!"

"I'll give you half," was her father's offer. *Seriously?*

"HALF? I bought the last one. Why can't you buy this one?" I argued.

"Cause, I don't have it."

"Fine! So when can you bring your half?"

"Next Friday," he said.

"What time?"

"I don't know. I get there when I get there," he snapped.

CLICK! I hung up.

"Idiot!" It seemed as if his disposition was becoming more and more frigid each time we spoke...

"Nishi, do you know where those ashes in the garage came from?" Grams asked one evening.

"No, but I saw it too and I was gonna ask you about it," I responded.

"This is the second time now that I've gone out there to sweep it up and I ain't gonna keep cleaning up somebody else's mess," Grams vented.

"Did you ask my mother?"

"No. Not yet, but I am."

Later that evening after my mother arrived home from work, Grams approached her.

"Gladys do you know how those ashes got in the garage?"

"No," she answered in a calm tone.

"Now I dun asked everybody in this house and no one knows a thing. Somebody got to know something!" The room remained quiet.

"I want you to ask Ethon when he comes in," Grams said.

"I knew that shit was coming!" my mother responded, sucking her teeth. "Now why does it have to be him? Every time something goes wrong around here, it's always Ethon." my mother said, lashing out.

"What's wrong with you ASSHOLE?" Grams yelled. "I didn't say anything about him doin' it, I just want you to ask him if he knows anything about it. Shit, for all I know somebody could be tryin' to burn my damn house down."

My mother ignored Grams' unimaginable statement and descended to her basement apartment. Although, I agreed with Grams, I remained silent and over the next several days I watched for signs of peculiar behavior and it wasn't long before the mystery began to unravel.

After returning home from one of Sara's demanding therapeutic visits one afternoon, I heard the backyard door slam. This spiked my curiosity. I quickly undressed Sara, placed her in the crib for a peaceful nap and like a country bumpkin yearning for some collard greens and pickled pigs feet, I scurried down to the kitchen.

While peeping through the back kitchen window, Ethon, who obviously assumed that he was home alone was rolling up some newspapers and setting them afire. *What the hell is he doin'?* He then raised his burning chronicle to his face and held it there for a short period of time. The flames began to burn out of control. Within moments, he stomped on the paper and continued to do so until the fire died out.

This menace, unaware that I was observing his firefighting technique, exited the garage and rushed into the house. I ran like a bat out of hell and hid in the dining room behind the china cabinet. As I peeped around the wall to see where he had gone, I saw him removing handfuls of old newspaper from our storage closet. *What's the rush? And is that a stem in his hand?* I looked harder. Sure was. Senor

Cabeza de Cracko was at it again. Instead of using the Bunsen burner, he was now using some old newspapers as his flame thrower and a glass stem in lieu of a full-fledged pipe. Before I could make sense of all this, he returned to the garage and again, rolled up an old Bill Buetel article. Someone's gotta put this clown's act to an end. He got high in front of me and I'll be damned if he does this shit around my little brother.

"Grams, I know who's leaving the burned paper in the garage," I reported later that same evening.

"Who is it?" she inquired.

"Your son in-law."

"You kiddin' me?" she said in amazement.

"Nope, I'm dead serious! I got home around twelve thirty today and caught him."

"But why is he burning paper though?" Grams frowned.

"I think he's on crack again because I also saw him with a glass stem in his hand."

"Stem?" Grams naively voiced.

"Yeah, a stem. You know the glass like tube that is usually attached to the pipe itself?"

"Honey, I have no idea what you're talkin' about," she stated.

"Well anyway, this is how he smokes it - I should have known though." I shook my head in disgust.

"What do you mean you should have known?" Grams tore opened her bag of roasted peanuts.

"Remember the day when he had the accident with the van?" I started out.

"Yeah?"

"Well, when I went outside to see how bad the damage was, there was this funny smell coming from inside of the van. I really didn't want to say anything, knowing how defensive my mother can be – so I left it alone, but I had a feeling that it was crack then. The smell was sweet with a slight burning scent. A SMELL THAT I WILL NEVER FORGET!"

"Hmmmm!" Grams muttered while shelling her peanuts at the kitchen table.

"I don't know about you, but I'm going to ask for my motorcycle key back. Especially since the radio's been stolen from the van and just last week, Donald mentioned to me that he saw me riding my bike one morning."

"You gotta be kiddin' me? You mean your motorcycle?"

"Yep! And I told him that it must have been someone else with a bike like mine, but he was certain that it was my bike."

"Well somebody was ridin' it," Grams said.

"Yeah, Ethon," I stated.

"Well, all I have to say is that's what you get for letting him ride it in the first place 'cause now he thinks that he can ride it any time he wants to."

"That's bull! The first time I knew about it 'cause I gave him the key, but to just ride it without my permission? No, I don't think so!"

"Well I guess your mother gave him her set then, 'cause he damn sure been on it." She paused and shook her head. "That don't make no kind'a sense. He's gonna have to go!" Grams seriously stated.

Things got hot later that night.

"Mommy can you come here for a minute please?" I shouted towards the basement's entrance.

"What is it?" she asked, approaching the doorway, still half dressed in her postal uniform.

"Umm... I need my key back," I said uneasily.

Grams silently sat at the kitchen table, awaiting my mother's response.

"For what? You never asked for it before?" she responded suspiciously.

"Did Ethon ride my bike one day last week?"

"Maybe! Maybe not! And since you want your key back, I want my van keys back too,"she hissed. What was her purpose for defending this loser? I dug down in my pants pocket and handed her the keys and the remote.

"He's ridden it before so what's your point?" she asked while adding the second set of van keys to her key ring.

"Mommy, my point is that he's been riding my bike without my permission. And what if the cops catch him? Did you two ever think about that?"

"AND?" she asked, raising her voice.

"AND MY ASS! THAT'S YOUR DAUGHTER'S BIKE, NOT HIS!" Grams shouted. It was now two against one. "And another thing, he's the one who's been leaving those ashes in my f^@%kin' garage. What is he tryin' to do burn the house down?"

"And how do you know this?" my mother asked in a negative tone.

"Ain't his ass home now? Go and ask him," Grams ordered.

"Ethon can you come up here for a minute please?" my mother called down to him.

I looked at Grams, knowing that the situation was about to intensify, but I was simply looking out for my family and this was the same individual that had contributed to our family's narcotic nightmare several years ago; I wasn't about to let that happen again.

As he climbed the basement steps, I asked my mother for my duplicate key again. She ignored me and queried him in a way that she was certain he'd say no.

"Some ashes were found in the garage. I know that you don't know anything about that, right?"

"Ashes? Nahh," he snickered in an impish manner.

"Ethon, so you haven't been taking my old newspapers from this closet here and using it to burn your drugs?" Grams asked, cutting straight to the chase. His face slightly hardened and again, he denied the accusations.

"Nishi said..." *Ahhh shit! She's about to put me on the spot. HERE WE GO!* "Nishi said that she saw you with the pipe in your hand," she disclosed.

"No Grams. The stem," I clarified.

"The pipe. The stem. Whatever! Anyway, she saw you," Grams made them aware.

At this point he looked up at me. I raised my left eyebrow and twisted my lips as to say WHAT NOW?

"It ain't true Moms!" he attempted to convince my grandmother as he stood one step down behind my mother.

"How are you gonna stand there and lie like that?" I asked, becoming irritated.

"Nishi. You just tryin' to start sum' ten (something) but I'm not havin' it," Ethon responded, this time without the smirk.

"Start something? You started the day my grandmother let you move in here. First my dog disappears how many times? Then my daughter takes a fall down these same steps and 'til this day, NOT ONE OF YOU have come to me and had the decency to apologize for moving the damn stick. I'm just sick of your f^@%kin' shit! "At this point I was boiling and I didn't give a damn about him anymore.

"You know what Nishi? You aint nut'tin but a bitch!" he claimed.

"Bitch?" I laughed.

"You left your bitches in prison and don't think for one moment that we don't hear the fighting and arguing that goes on down here – like we heard the other night. What was that big BOOM noise? Probably the reason why she called the cops on your ass. I don't know why she didn't let them take you back and cage you like the animal that you are. PUNK ASS!" I vented.

"Gladys!" Ethon tapped my mother on her shoulder to get her undivided attention. "Your daughter aint nut'tin but a f^@%kin' bitch and she needs to check herself or I will!"

Spoken like a true abusive man. Forever thinking of hitting a woman. Bring it on ass wipe! I was waiting for this vindictive scum to set it off, and he was on the staircase too?

"MOTHERF#^@%*&! YOU AIN'T GONNA DO SHIT, BUT WHAT YOU NEED AND EVENTUALLY WILL DO IS GET THE F#^@ OUT OF MY GRANDMOTHER'S HOUSE!" I shouted. He then advanced onto the kitchen level and leaned towards me.

"Like I said, YOU – AINT – DOIN' – SHIT!" I stepped to my opponent.

"And like I said, you aint nut'tin but a bitch!" he repeated.

"F^@%kin' dope fiend!" I said while shifting in his direction.

We were literally standing inches away from one another now.

"Grams you better get her!" my mother calmly stated.

"Get her for what? Everything she's sayin' is right," Grams supported my argument.

"Whatever! But if she gets hurt don't say anything to me," my mother surprisingly said.

"WHAT?" I voiced in utter dismay. I looked at my mother to see if she was really serious.

"I HOPE SHE KNOCKS HIS ASS DOWN THOSE F^@%KIN' STEPS. SHOW HIM HOW MY GRAND BABY FELT!" Grams yelled. Although Sara was really her great grand, Grams sometimes shortened her title. I guess it made her feel younger.

"You act like a man! You get hit like a man!" Ethon threatened.

"Sssssst!" I sucked my teeth. "Like I said you ain't gonna do shit. Mommy gimme my keys!" I demanded.

"I ain't givin' you shit! Didn't you say something about selling it anyway? Well, it's mine now." Again, my mother responded strangely. I frowned upon her crazy words and just looked at her.

"How is that motorcycle yours Gladys?" Grams asked.

"I bought it right?" she bragged.

"Now you know that's not right!" Grams exclaimed.

"Well, a lot of things around here ain't right but like I said, I bought it."

That evening I never got to kick his ass, but Lord knows I wanted to. And sadly, I didn't get my key back either.

Days later, my mother ransacked my room looking for my motorcycle title. While doing so, she broke my stereo case and took a few pieces of jewelry she'd bought for me as a child. Grams and I couldn't believe it; she had gone berserk. She got away with the jewelry, but never found the title. My intuition told me that she would try something senseless, so quick-thinking me hid it in one of my speakers. As Grams and I examined my messy room, I voiced a deep thought.

"She's actin' just like him – A CRACKHEAD!"

"You right about that," Grams agreed.

Little did I know my bike had been kicked over and was now laying on its side in the garage.

After seeing the results of her daughter's very disturbed behavior, Grams had no other choice but to evict her. Grams told me that her decision was painful, especially since Lee was subjected to the displacement.

Friday evening, around 6:30 the doorbell rang.

"Goodnight!" he greeted me.

"Hey!" I responded.

"I tried to put mo' (more), but this is all I could do," he said, handing me an envelope. As I proceeded to open it, he struck up a conversation.

"Where are you puppies?"

"Gone," I quickly responded while opening the sealed envelope.

"A money order?" I looked at him.

"Yeah - what's wrong wit dat?" he asked.

He's never given me a money order and this idiot spelled my name wrong.

"Whatever! Anyway - thanks." I reinserted the certified funds. *Let me just be thankful.*

"Where's me dottuh (daughter)?" he asked.

"She's in the back with my grandmother."

"Go and get she so I can say Hi." I called Sara to the front.

As she came running towards us, Teddy kneeled.

"Hi Mommy!" he revealed his nicotine stained teeth. I once told him to gargle with Clorox to brighten up his smile, but evidently he disregarded my suggestion.

"How's daddy's little swit'hat (sweetheart)? Gimme kiss!" Sara slowly backed up and looked at him as if he were crazy. With that look he knew that he wasn't going to get a kiss, so he gently grabbed her and took one.

"So full of shit! If she's so much of your sweetheart then why haven't you seen her in how long?" I mumbled.

"Sssssst!" he sucked his teeth. "Here - take she!" he handed Sara over to me.

"How's she eye?" he tried to act like a concerned parent.

"It's there," I shrewdly responded.

Teddy snickered and pushed the screen door open to leave.

"Later!" He said as he attempted to close the door behind him.

"Wait! When are we gonna see you again?" I jammed the door with my foot.

"I don't know." he then turned, ran down the steps and jumped into his idling van. "I'LL CALL YOU!" he shouted from the van. *Whatever!* I closed the door and headed up to my room with Sara.

"NISHI WAS THAT TEDDY?" Grams projected her voice.

"Yeah."

"Did he bring you any money?" she boldly questioned me. I paused before I could answer.

"Yeah, why?" I asked.

"Nothing. I just wanted to know." Grams and I were close and all, but she had crossed the line now.

"Nishi?" She called again.

"Yeah?"

"Come here for a minute. I wanna ask you somethin'." I about-faced and descended the staircase.

"Yeah?" I said as I entered the kitchen.

"I got a little problem with my taxes this year and my tax man said that if I could find a dependent then it would help me out a great deal. So can I claim Sara as a dependent?"

"How when I'm claiming her on my welfare case?" I asked, becoming somewhat upset.

"What do you mean how? Just give me her social security number."

"No."

"Why not?" she snapped.

"Because I just told you and plus, they already found out about my temp jobs. And what's gonna happen when they find out about this? I don't need those people asking me any more questions than what they already have."

"Well, the way I look at it – if you're living here in my house I should be able to claim whoever I want to," she concluded.

"How can you, when you`re not even taking care of her?"

"Like I said. You live here with your daughter so I should be able to claim her."

"Well - I don't know how," I said and walked away.

She got some damn nerve trying to muscle my daughter's personal information out of me for her own problems.

Approximately one month later, the treacherous two were in their beginning stages of relocating. As Ethon loaded her van, she and Lee packed his car. Yep, not long after our falling out, my mother bought him a car.

"Nishi I think you need to talk to your mother before she makes the biggest mistake of her life," Evelyn stated. She was concerned about her sister's well-being. It just so happened she visited on the same day they were moving out.

"Please! She's a grown woman. She knows what she's doin'." I rolled my eyes.

"No she doesn't. She has no idea what she's about to get herself and Lee into," my aunt fretted.

"I'm not sayin' a word. If you wanna talk to her, that's your business," I responded.

"That man is gonna kill her out there. If he was brave enough to kick her ass in her own mother's house

then what do you think he's going to do to her out there?"
Evelyn continued to stress herself out.

"Look. I already told you, she's a grown woman and
that's her business."

I shut the conversation down, grabbed Sara and
went up to my room. Yeah, it was killing me to see her
leaving with this mad man, but what could I do? She had
already showed and told me in so many words that I was
her enemy. This was her life.

———————————

Months later, Teddy remembered us because he
unexpectedly came by with another money order.

"What's up with these money orders?" I asked him.

"No special reason. It's just that I want prŭf
(proof)," he replied.

"Proof for what?"

"I don't know. You never know."

"What's that supposed to mean? Do you think I'm going to take you to court for child support?" I asked him.

"Like I said, you never know gyul."

"First of all Teddy, I always talk to you about things before they get ugly, but for some reason you never come clean. Like for instance, when I asked you if MooMoo was pregnant - I asked you twice before I smacked your ass. And you even lied about havin' children. Now how screwed up is that? And leave it up to you - you were a bachelor, which is why we're in this situation today. I've never given you a reason to lie to me; I've always dealt with you right and hoped that someday you'll do the same."

He held his head down throughout my entire lecture.

"Nishi I know. She's dee one that's makin' me give you dee money orders. She asked me if me was givin' you anyting for dee baby and I tell she yes and then she asked me how much?" Teddy confessed.

"And you answered her, right?" I presumed.

"Yeah. So she could get off me back. She said whenever I give you money that I must let she know."

"Let her know for what?" I frowned.

"I guess she wanna make sho' (sure) of dee amount - I don't know."

"With the first money order I knew that YOU weren't the one who filled it out," I explained.

"How?" he questioned.

"Because my name was misspelled and the signature wasn't yours."

"Damn gyul, you see everyting (everything)."

"That's right! But I wasn't about to get into all that when you brought it that night."

"Nishi, believe me I don't like dee way this whole ting is goin'. Just don't be mad at me plĭz (please)?" He seemed sincere.

"Whatever Teddy!"

"For real. I promise you, it'll get better."

"Oh, I know. I can tell," I said sarcastically.

He pulled me into a bear hug. God I love this man. Why can't things just work out for us? He held up my chin to kiss me.

"No! I'm not kissing you!" I jumped back.

"Plĭz (please) Nishi? I missed you so much. Don't do me like this plĭz (please)," he begged, and like a fool in love, I kissed him.

"Mmmmm!" I jumped back - pushing him away.

"What's wrong wit you gyul?"

"Nothing. It's time for you to leave now," I told him. Being in love is a motherf#^@%*& and it will make you do some really stupid things.

"Didn't you leave your van running?" I asked as I looked at his van through the front window.

"No. For what?"

"You did last time."

"Because I had some whaye (somewhere) to go, but tonight I came to spend time wit you and me dottuh," he stated.

"Exactly! And on that note let me get her."

As I went for Sara, he made himself comfortable on the living room couch. That night, it felt as if we were a real family.

Despite what my mother had done and said to me in the past, we managed to move on but deep in my heart I knew things would never be the same between us two. She'd visit us almost every weekend for hours, but lately she's been coming straight after work. Ethon would call to check up on her and soon after, she'd leave. Her actions were suspicious and I sensed that something was wrong.

"Every time I see that van it looks worse and worse," Grams noticed.

"Mmmm!" I murmured.

"I'm just so damn glad that it's no longer in my name," she exhaled.

"Did you see the front bumper? It was all pushed in," I informed her.

"No, I only saw the side door. It didn't look like that shit when you and Gladys drove it. Boy oh boy, I don't know why she LET'N THAT MAN BRING HER DOWN LIKE THAT!" Grams shook her head in disgust.

With Sara's therapy sessions down to only twice a month, I searched for a full - time permanent position. I filled out many applications and went on several interviews. Looking for a full-time job WAS a full time job and things got even more real when I noticed, NO BRAIDS OR DREADLOCKS in bold letters at the bottom of one particular application. Or receiving notices in the mail stating, "We appreciate your interest in our company. However, at this time we have chosen other candidates that we consider to be more suitable for the position."

I concluded would have to cut my locks and definitely resume my education. But how? I had no money and I no longer had the van to drive. Books were expensive and to top it off, I was now paying rent to Grams – per her request. There was no way that I could come up with enough money for all of this. I decided to ask Teddy if he could at least assist me with the weekly babysitting fee.

During one of my mother's weekend visits, I asked her if I could borrow the van for a few minutes. Coincidently, Renee` happened to stop by that same night. She took the ride with me.

"Nish, you think he's home?" Renee' asked me.

"I don't know, hopefully." His van was the first thing we saw after turning onto his block.

"So what are you gonna do - ring his bell?"

"I really don't want to cause I don't feel like being bothered with the MooMoo, but I guess I'm gonna have to."

"Well, you better do something, 'cause I'm not going to sit out here in front of this building like we're on a stakeout or some shit." Renee joked.

Four minutes later, who exits the building?

"There he is right there!" The 20/20 vision having Renee' sighted my baby's daddy immediately. With his keys dangling from his hand, Teddy casually walked towards his van. In only three steps, daddy long legs was already at his vehicle.

"TEDDY!" I jumped out and yelled. He looked straight at me and kept on walking. I couldn't believe it.

"TEDDY!" I yelled again. This time he didn't even look at me. He inserted his key and unlocked the door to his van. I ran and caught up to him before he could get in.

"Teddy, what's wrong with you? I know you heard me calling you." I reached to touch his hand.

"Don't touch me gyul!" He snatched away.

"What's your damn problem?" I returned the attitude.

"Look, just lĭv (leave) me alone!"

"Leave you alone? I'll leave you alone alright. I came here to talk to you about the babysitting for Sara," I explained.

"What about it?"

"I'm going back to school and I wanna know if you're gonna help pay for it?" I asked.

"Look. I don't have any money," he said as he pulled his door open.

"WATCH WHAT YOU'RE F^@%KIN' DOIN'!" I shouted. As he swung open his driver's side door, the edge of it hit me in the face.

"So move from dey (there)!" he ordered.

"You know what? You're such a f^@%kin' idiot," I nudged him in his protruding forehead.

Boy why did I do that. He jumped out of his van, grabbed my hand and started bending my fingers back.

"KEEP YOU F^@%KIN' HAH'NZ (HANDS) TO YOU SELF!" he yelled.

"F^@% you and get off of me!" I kicked him in his shin.

"Go home gyul!" Teddy angrily stated.

"I ain't going nowhere until I know that you're gonna help me with the babysitting."

"Where's dee money that me give you?" he asked.

"You gotta be kiddin' me. I know you ain't even talkin' about that measly old seventy-five dollars that you gave me three months ago. THREE MONTHS AGO! Let's see, what is that twenty-five dollars each month?" I argued.

"I don't have any money okay?" he said while sitting in the driver's seat and holding onto his door handle. I couldn't believe the way that he was acting.

"NISH!" Renee' yelled from my mother's van.

"What?"

"Forget it! You standing there arguing with the man ain't gonna make it any better." She was right, but his attitude is what really got to me.

"What if your ass ends up in court?" POW! Teddy hit me in the face.

"Oh hell no! BITCH!" I shouted. Never totally getting inside of his van, Teddy sat with one of his legs hanging over the edge. BOOM! I slammed the door on his ankle and backed away from the van. He hopped out swinging. By now we had drawn a small crowd. Three young men, about our age walked up just as Teddy and I started our boxing match.

"Yo, you can't be hittin' on a woman like that!" one guy said.

"You don't know she. She can take it," Teddy responded. SWOOOSH! Teddy hurled a punch at me.

I ducked and hit him with an upper cut.

"My man's right. She fights like a dude," another spectator shouted.

Teddy stumbled into the side of his building. These guys were no longer interested in breaking us up, they were now street side viewers, along with Renee', who was now standing outside of my mother's van.

"I'M GONNA KILL YOU GYUL!" Teddy shouted.

SWOOOSH!

He hurled another punch. It landed slightly above my left eye. This pissed me off, so I charged him like a heifer with mad cow's disease. The punk's knees buckled and he went down, but instead of going down by himself - he dragged me with him. I wrestled to get out of his grip, but was unsuccessful.

With no more punches being thrown, the three men then separated us.

"PUSSY!" I shouted.

The biggest of the three guys held me with one of his arms and at the same time managed to hold Teddy at a distance.

"That's enough! I'm not gonna stand here and watch this go on any longer. Now what kind of man would I be if I did that?" he chuckled.

"LET THE BITCH GO!" I yelled.

"Yo shorty, you went for yours and you did good too!" the big bouncer type guy said.

"I'm glad she ain't my girl, 'cause fightin' her is like fightin' a dude," another one said.

"Nishi - look!" Renee' pointed to the ground.

"He pulled your hair out!" she shrieked as she picked up my locks. During the tussle, the bastard pulled my hair and on the ground, lay a handful of my locks.

"P-t-u-u-u-u-u-!" I spat on Teddy. Unfortunately, some of my saliva hit the big guy.

"HEY, I REALLY THINK THAT YOU NEED TO CALM DOWN FOR REAL NOW!" the big guy warned me.

"Man-n-n, you need to make up with your girl, 'cause it seems like she's ready for another round with you," one guy said.

"F^@% she! Let she go!" Teddy said while straightening up his jacket.

"Nah-h-h son, I don't think you really wanna do that," one guy laughed.

On the way home Renee' could not stop talking about the fight.

"Nishi you fight like a man! You should'a seen yourself – ducking and weaving! I couldn't believe my eyes and those guys were laughing throughout the entire thing. Wait 'til I tell Paul this one! He's gonna bust out laughin'!"

Without Teddy's help, I went back to college. However, after three months of dropping Sara off at the babysitter at 7:00 in the morning, then having to wait on those buses in the freezing cold to attend classes at a college out in Coney Island and finally, making sure that Sara made it to her weekly scheduled therapy sessions, I was exhausted. So instead of me trying to pursue my education in health once again, I now had an interest in law enforcement. On the NYPD exam I scored 97 and on the Department of Corrections exam I scored 92.

NYPD contacted me first. I passed their medical exam with flying colors. While waiting to receive word on the upcoming physical fitness date, they initiated my background check.

For weeks, I waited to hear back from them and finally, I got a call from my investigator.

"Hi Nishelle, it's Detective Abberton. How's everything?" My investigator was a short, cool, Irish woman. Probably the smallest person in her department, but don't sleep on her because she was well respected.

"Everything's fine," I responded.

"Okay, I have some good news and some bad news. Which one do you want first?"

For a moment my mind froze. I took a deep breath.

"Alright. Let's start with the good news," I decided.

"Okay, most of your paper work came back and it looks good, but unfortunately, the Housing, Transit and City Police departments have all merged which created a problem for you."

"And why is that?" I questioned calmly.

"Not only have they merged, but the last two lists have been combined with yours which pushes you further back on the list. So now, instead of you being in the "A" band or top hundred, you'd be somewhere in the thousands," she explained.

"I can't believe this."

"I know Nishelle. It's horrible, but I had to tell you."

"So how long do you think that it'll be before I get called?"

"I have no idea, but at this rate, probably no time soon."

There was a moment of silence on the phone.

"In any event, I have your paper work here and if anything changes, I'll give you a call. Good luck Nishelle!"

After hanging up from the detective, I sat for a few minutes in silence. Once again, the system failed me. I was convinced that this was their way of weeding out the minorities. Fed up and just tired of the drama, I thought of a plan B...

Weeks later, Sara and I relocated to Pennsylvania to stay with a cousin. Down there I also took and passed the police exam, but unlike New York, Philadelphia's Police Dept. contacted me within weeks. Again, I did well and was told by my investigator that I had a very good chance of being recruited for the next academy class. My job now was to get that requested paperwork back to them in a timely fashion.

Their investigation process was the same, very thorough. And for the simple fact that I wasn't a Philly native, I had to take the trip back to the Big Apple to collect the necessary documents in person...

"REMINISCING"

TAKE A FEW MOMENTS AND THINK BACK

REMEMBER THOSE DAYS WHEN YOU LACKED

FRIENDS WERE THERE OF COURSE, THE KIN

THINK HOW THEY HELPED YOU THROUGH THICK
AND THIN

STRUGGLING WAS A PART OF THE GAME

YOU, YOURSELF WAS THE ONLY ONE TO BLAME

LIFE IS WHAT YOU MAKE IT, PROBLEMS MAY
OCCUR

REMEMBER THOSE WHO HAD OPEN ARMS AND
DOORS

"Well, I guess you know by now that Ethon no longer has his car?" Grams began to fill me in.

"No, I didn't know that," I replied.

"Your mother didn't tell you? He totaled it. And Lee was with him when it happened.

"I could tell that she wanted to tell me something while I was there, but when he came home she changed the entire conversation."

"Well what was she sayin'?" Grams asked me.

"She mentioned that she was tired and if she knew then what she knew now, it would have been a different story," I relayed. "I asked her what did she mean by that and just when she was about to tell me, he walked in and I left right after he came in. So tell me about this accident Grams."

"Honey, all I know is that he totaled the car and Lee was with him when it happened." Grams revealed.

"Well, hopefully before I go back to Philly she'll tell me what happened. And Lee…"

"What about Lee?" Grams interrupted, looking at me sideways.

"He had this sign up on his bedroom door and it said, "Stop smoking that stinking stuff in my room.

"What stinkin' stuff?" Grams frowned.

"I don't know," I replied, "but I'm gonna find out before I leave." I made certain.

After running around for three whole days, I successfully retrieved all of the necessary documents.

"Hello Mommy. What are you doin'?" I called her one evening.

"Sittin' here talking to my son. Why, what's up?

"Nothing. I just called to see what you were up to and to see if you wanted to take a ride over here to Grams'?"

"When? Right now?" she asked.

"Yeah." I responded.

"Well I can't right now because Ethon has the van."

"Oh..alright then."

"But you can come over here!" she excitedly suggested.

"Mommy please," I huffed. "You know that I can't stand to be around that man."

"Please," she confidently retorted. "He ain't comin' home no time soon."

"How do you know?" I asked, still skeptical.

"Cause I just do."

"Nah-h-h," I said, sticking to my premonition, "I think I'll pass on this one."

"No come!" she insisted. "I'm tellin' you. He's probably gonna be gone for the rest of the night. Just take a taxi, I'll pay for it!"

I sighed, shaking my head. "Alright. I'll call you when I'm on my way."

Thirty minutes later, I was knocking on her front door.

"NISHI, HOW MUCH IS THE CAB?" my mother shouted from the top floor window.

"TWELVE DOLLARS!" I hollered back.

She was renting the second level of a two family house, which just so happened to be owned by Ethon's niece.

"Here!" She threw the money down along with her house keys.

After paying the taxi driver and entering the house, she and Lee greeted me at the top of the staircase.

"Hey Sara!" She grabbed her and squeezed her hard. "How's granny's pretty little girl?"

"What's up with this crazy ass cat?" I asked, shooing the very energetic feline away from me.

"What's wrong? You don't like Byron? He's a good cat. Shit, he catches more mice and roaches than those sticky traps." My mother praised her animal.

"But why is he running around like he's crazy?" I asked.

This cat had issues. He would dash from one side of the apartment and back, jump on the kitchen table, run across the bed a few times and then back into the living room. Then from the opposite corner of the living room, he'd sit and stare at you. WHAT THE HELL?

"Byron's cool," she laughed, trying to convince me.
"Lee. Come and get your cat before I kick the shit out of
it," I said. *Creepy ass cat.*

"So how's the postal business?" I initiated some
small talk.

"It's okay. I'm still a sub, but I'll be a regular soon."

I turned and saw that "Stop smoking that stinking
stuff in my room" sign on Lee's door again.

"Mommy what's that about?" I asked.

"What?" She followed the path of my eyes.

"Oh, Ethon was smokin' one day and I guess Lee
didn't want to smell it so he put that up."

She laughed it off, but deep in my mind, I wondered
what could possibly smell so bad to make a young child
display such a disturbing sign. Although she made the sign

seem like a joke, I sensed that something else was behind this story.

"Mommy is he smoking crack in front of Lee?" I asked her, getting straight to the point.

I had no time to beat around the bush because the Philadelphia P.D. was waiting on my documents. From her hesitation, I already knew what her answer was going to be. She took a deep breath.

"I don't know really, but one day when I got home from work the sign was there. I asked both of them what was going on and Ethon's reply was that he simply smoked a few cigarettes, but Lee kept saying that it was a stinky cigarette. I didn't push the issue because I didn't want to get into it with Ethon."

"What do you mean that you didn't want to push the issue?" I snapped. "Mommy this is your son and if he's tellin' you that something is out of the norm then you should look into it. Do you want him to experience the whole crack - dope scene thing like I did?"

"No," my mother said, growing exasperated. "But Ethon gets so upset when I ask him things, or just even talking to him sets him off. Sometimes he gets on my nerves to the point where I just want him to disappear forever."

"What happened with that social work job that he applied for?" I asked.

"He didn't get it."

"Why? What happened?"

"Because he came up pregnant."

"What? What are you talking about?" Her statement confused me.

"Nish, I know the fool is back on drugs and when the people called him to come in for an interview, he froze up. I asked him what was wrong and that's when he told me that he is using drugs again."

"Okay, so that still doesn't explain how he came up 'pregnant'," I impatiently stated.

"Wait! I'm getting to that part." She held up her hand, signaling me to be patient. I sat back, crossing my arms, waiting for the punch line.

"He took some of my piss in to them."

"You're lying!" I widened my eyes in amazement. We sat silently for a few seconds. I couldn't believe what she had just said.

"So what are you telling me is that you were pregnant and lost the baby?"

"Yep. I miscarried that one too. You remember when you and Grams said that y'all heard a big boom in the basement one day?"

"Yeah?"

"Well that was the day when he got really mad at me, picked me up and threw me to the floor."

"Huuuuh!" I sighed, shaking my head.

"The next week, I started havin' a lot of cramps and spotting," she explained.

"So you KNEW that he was using drugs before you moved out?"

"He wasn't abusing it though," she said, trying to defend him. "Like I said, he was just smoking it in a cigarette."

"What difference does it make? Cigarette. Pipe. It's still crack Mommy!" I clarified.

"You're right," she said shamefully. I couldn't believe this shit.

She knew that he was back on drugs, yet she turned against me knowing that I was right all along.

"So what about you?" I asked her. "Are you on it again too?"

"No. But I'm not going to lie; I've smoked it in a cigarette a couple of times though."

"For what Mommy? Didn't you have enough?" She really struck a nerve. "Like I said do you want Lee to go through the same shit that I went through?" I could feel myself getting upset.

"He's not. I only did it a few times; since then I've stopped."

"I'm tellin' you now. If you get back on that shit like before, you're on your own!"

"I know Nish," my mother sighed. "I'm just so tired of him and his shit. My van looks like hell and every time I turn around, he's banging it up more."

"And that's another thing," I said, changing the subject, "what's this about him totaling his car?"

"I see 'your mother' told you huh?" She sarcastically referred to Grams.

"Yeah she mentioned it to me," I confirmed. "So what happened?"

"Paranoid ass Ethon thinks, for some reason, that I'm seeing someone behind his back," she explained. "So one day he decided to come to Harlem and spy on me as I did my route. I guess after he saw that everything was cool, he left. But according to Lee, he left in a hurry. The accident happened not too far from my postal station too. He hit this old white man from behind. I think the accident report said something about the old man having a heart attack at the time."

"Are you serious?" I asked.

"Yep...and Ethon's car looked like shit. Nothing really happened to the old man's car; his rear bumper was just torn off."

"Shit - that's ENOUGH!" I said in disgust. Just picturing the accident turned my stomach. "Poor Lee! My little brother must have been scared like hell."

"G-i-r-r-l! My baby told me that he was flying down the street when it happened. He said that Ethon kept saying that he had to pick up an important package."

"What important package? A crack vial?" I smirked.

"Probably! What else would cause him to be so much in a rush?"

My mother was a sad example as a parent. This was the same man that, some twelve years ago, showed me how to cook and smoke crack, and now he's trying to kill my little brother with his crazy ass driving. This destructive person had no purpose in life.

"This wasn't the first time he had Lee cruisin' the streets with him either," my mother admitted. "A few weeks before the accident he had some lady in the car and Lee told me that he kissed her."

"Wait! While Lee was in the car?" I surprisingly asked.

"Uh huh. Lee said that he was sleeping in the back seat, but they didn't realize that he woke up."

"You got my mouth dry with all this talkin'. What do you have here to drink?" I asked.

"VITAMINS!" Lee projected his voice into the living room. My mother and I looked at each other.

"WHAT?" I shouted back.

"Vitamins!" He repeated effortlessly.

For an eight year old he had a very mellow and mature demeanor about himself. He seemed so much older and his deep voice made everything he said even more convincing.

"Come here Lee!" I called my little brother. He slowly approached the living room.

"Yah!" He said as he grew closer to me.

"Why did you say 'vitamins'?" I asked him.

"Because that's what I eat when I'm hungry when mommy's not home," he replied. "I eat vitamins and when I get thirsty, I mix them with water to make it taste like Kool-Aid."

UNBELIEVABLE! My heart dropped.

My only brother that I helped raised, and who had just turned eight in June, was over dosing on chewable vitamins.

"Stop lyin'!" My mother blurted.

"I'm not lyin'," Lee kept to his admission.

"Why vitamins though? Why don't you just ask Ethon to make you something to eat?"

I continued to interrogate my little brother.

"I do, but he always tells me to leave him alone and wait until Mommy gets home."

"Alright Lee, you can go back and play with Sara now," I told him.

As I turned to view my mother, hoping to get a reasonable explanation from her, she again dropped her head in shame. Without saying another word, I headed towards her kitchen.

"Mommy where are you going?" Sara jumped up and followed me.

"In the kitchen to get somethin' to drink."

"I want something to drink too," she said. I opened the refrigerator and just as Lee said, there was nothing to drink. All I saw was an opened can of condensed milk and one onion.

"Mommy come here!" Quietly my mother entered the kitchen area.

"I know what you callin' me for," she said before I could even jump down her throat.

"Lee's not lyin'. There's absolutely nothing here to drink or to eat in this fridge. What's goin' on Mommy?"

"Nishi I have so many bills to pay and every time that I turn around, parking tickets are coming in the mail and if not that, he's asking me for more allowance," she explained.

"ALLOWANCE?" I screamed. "You must be crazy! That's a grown ass man."

"I give it to him so he'll leave me alone. One day he ripped off my uniform shirt when I refused to give it to him."

"But Mommy that's exactly what he wants you to do. Give up your money so he can go and get high. You have a son to take care of and here you are supportin' this loser in every way. Why are you subjecting yourself to this bullshit?"

She looked as if she wanted to break down and cry.

"The corner store, is it still open?" I changed the subject, alleviating some of the pressure.

"I don't know. Why?" She managed to say while wiping away the tears.

"Because you need something in your refrigerator other than condensed milk and one onion."

Lucky for her my public assistance case was successfully transferred to Philly and I had just gotten my first set of food stamps for the month.

"Sara. Mommy's going to the store. I'm going to bring back some chips and juice for you and Lee okay?"

Before stepping out, I made sure that my daughter was comfortable and then made a quick run to the grocery store. Within minutes, I returned with three full grocery bags.

"This should hold you for a while," I said as I unpacked the bags. I bought three different kinds of cold cereal, juice, two gallons of milk and some after school snacks for Lee. Although she never thanked me that night for the food, the main thing was that Lee was eating right...

On the way back to Philly, all I could think of was my mother and Lee. *How were they surviving? What type of life will my brother have if she gets addicted to crack again? Who will raise him? Is he safe living under the same roof as that man who he was now calling daddy?* These are questions that I asked myself throughout the entire bus ride. Her situation really bothered me, especially the part about Lee's "vitamin juice."

I called her some days later to see how things were going. Everything was still the same, but during our conversation she finally thanked me for the groceries and expressed that she enjoyed our visit.

"Don't worry about it. I just better not hear anything about you being on drugs again!" I warned.

"You won't!" She assured me.

"Let me say Hi to Lee real quick." She called Lee to the phone.

"Hello?" he said in his customary low tone.

"Hey shorty. How's things?" I asked him.

"Fine."

"How's school?"

"Fine."

"You're not eatin' those vitamins anymore right?"

"No." Lee was not very big on talking. Like his REAL father, everything spoken was usually short and to the point. Even down to the "Yah" responses. "Yah" is how Comisario communicated the word "yes." Comi's Panamanian accent was very strong and Lee, obviously, had adopted the accent by nature.

It's just too bad that Comi could no longer visit his son. Shortly after Ethon's release, my mother told him not to come around anymore because his "father" was now home, meaning Ethon.

To make this situation worse, just moments into a visit with Lee, my mother pulled Comisario to the side and instructed him to never come around again. Seconds later, Ethon pulled up in the car my mother had bought for him.

Comi witnessed the offensive actions of his innocent son as he ran towards Ethon shouting "Daddy!

Daddy! You're home." So in essence, my mother ran Lee's REAL father off. Obviously, Comisario (meaning commissioner/person in charge in Spanish) was not in control of THIS particular operation.

Some several years later, I paid Comi a visit at his auto body shop. He expressed to me how upset he was with my mother that day for cutting him out of his son's life like that. I understood and agreed with him, but what could I do?

"Alright. I'll talk to you soon okay?" I told my little brother.

"Yah."

"Let me speak to Mommy again before I hang up."

"M-O-M-M-MY!" He yelled.

"I got it!" I heard her say loudly in the background.

"Yeah Nish, you hang'n up now?" she asked.

"Yeah, because this call is gonna cost me a fortune. I'll call you some time next week." I told her.

"Kiss Sara for me okay?" she requested.

"Okay - bye."

"NI-S-H-I-I! I heard her yell my name as I attempted to place the receiver on the hook.

"Yeah, what is it?" I quickly placed the phone back to my ear.

"I just wanna let you know that I heard about the favor Grams asked you to do for her before you left."

"What? That tax thing?" I responded.

"Yeah and I just want you to know that she did use Sara as a dependent on her taxes."

"No she didn't because I never gave her Sara's social security number," I explained.

"Well obviously, she got it somehow because she mentioned that the dependent helped her get a refund back."

She provided me with the details.

"Well as soon as welfare or whoever starts asking me questions, I'm gonna tell it all..."

———————————————

Attending college directly after high school wasn't a bad idea, but when you're a drop out with little to no experience, you begin to feel it.

Biweekly, I collected one hundred and seventy dollars from welfare, which of course depleted after I paid rent and long distance phone calls. Things were hard in Philly too and now welfare was continuously inquiring about the father of my child so he'd be forced to pay child support. They warned me that if I didn't comply with the request, then my allowances would be minimized. This I couldn't afford so I gave them an address, a name and a birth date. Not too sure if it was Teddy's info, but I gave them something.

RING! RING! RING! RING!

"Nishi it's for you; it's your mother," my cousin stated after answering the phone.

"Thanks," I said as she handed the phone over to me.

"Hey mommy?" I spoke into the receiver.

"Hey! I got some good news," she spoke energetically.

"What kind of good news?"

"Well, I have two things to tell you. The first is that Ethon will most likely get deported."

"Yeah? What happened?" I asked.

"Of the many days he rode your bike, he obviously visited his parole officer and the asshole was seen riding it and they hit him with a violation, but get this, the driver's license that he had ..."

"Wait! He had a driver's license?" I interrupted her.

"Yeah, but it was of a dead man." She laughed out loud. She obviously found this situation to be very funny because she couldn't talk for laughing.

"Huh?" Of course, I was shocked. She now had my undivided attention. "And how did they find this out?" I asked my mother. "First of all, did YOU know this?"

"Yeah I did. But anyway, they traced the license back to him when the accident was reported. Apparently, his parole officer put two and two together when he realized that I was the same Gladys Maron that the car was registered in and that Ethon was living with. It took them some time, but they caught his ass. And when the idiot went back down there ..." She started to laugh again.

"Down where?" I asked.

"Downtown for his parole visit, they found that same driver's license on him and locked him up one time."

"So where is he now?"

"With the Department of Immigration on Varick Street in Manhattan."

"Well, it seems like you're gonna get your wish," I told her.

"I hope so. He calls me collect every day, but I never accept the charges."

"Knowing you, you will," I said without a doubt.

"No. I'm not."

"Whatever! So ET's (Ethon Thomas) really goin' home and what's the other good news?" I asked.

"I got mail for you from Grams and it's from The Department of Corrections. Do you want me to open it?"

"Yeah," I most certainly agreed. She began reading the letter aloud.

"Dear applicant, we would like to invite you to our interviewing session which will be held on August 22, 1994 at 8:00 A.M. sharp. Please wear business attire."

"We would like to invite you" was all I needed to hear. By the end of that call – my mind was set. Sara and I were going home. Once again, I got a shot to pursue a career in law enforcement and the opportunity to mend the cracked relationship with my mother...

Although it seemed things were moving along, there wasn't a day without drama. Just days after returning home, I opened the door of my mother's apartment to see a Solid Gold Tow Truck driver preparing to tow my mother's van away. Along with the tow truck driver, were two sheriff's vehicles and a cameraman that was videotaping the hook up.

"WAIT!" I yelled and ran across the street.

"What are you doin'? This is my mother's van."

"Miss, stand back please!" the officer ordered.

"What's goin' on?" I asked him. The cameraman aimed his camera at me.

"This van has several unpaid parking tickets on it." He presented me with a copy of the summonses.

"If your mother can furnish the full amount right now, then we'll release it and go about our business. If not, you'll have to stand back."

After looking at the list of tickets, I was sure that my mother didn't have this amount of money lying around in the house and I didn't have it either.

"Can you wait a minute while I call my mother?" I asked one of the Sheriffs.

"You can go ahead, but I can't promise you that we'll still be here by the time you return," he answered. Quickly, I ran back upstairs to call my mother and just as I thought – she didn't have the money.

"I called the sheriff's office. The van was towed to a parking lot in Bushwick and according to them the amount owed is five hundred dollars, plus storage and towing fees." My mother called me back later that morning with that information.

"Mommy are you serious?"

"Yeah! This motherfucker is gone and he's still causin' me problems," she vented.

"So what are you going to do?"

"Do you have any money that I can borrow from you 'til payday?" she asked.

"That depends. How much are you talking about?"

"Two hundred."

"TWO HUNDRED!" I repeated.

"Nish, if you can't do it, don't worry about it." I heard the disappointment in her voice.

"I mean - I can give you something, but not the full two." I really wanted to help her out of this jam.

"Will one fifty help?"

"Yeah - I'll find that extra fifty from somewhere. They close at six. Can you do me a favor and meet me down at the Sheriff's office, because I'll never make it in time if I have to come home and pick up the money?"

"Where is it?" I asked.

"It's the building directly across from the Department of Health on Worth Street."

"Alright. I'll leave as soon as Lee gets home from school, so I should get there well before five."

It took a lot of running, but with team effort we managed to make it to the Sheriff's office before closing time. After paying them, we headed for the lot, which wasn't too far from my mother's apartment.

Even though the misfit was gone, my mother was still being affected by his negative spirit. He'd call her every other day, leaving messages on the answering machine. Like an idiot, he'd ask her why she wouldn't accept his collect calls. He also had the nerve to tell her that he knew she was now seeing someone else. And she was.

Not long after Ethon's departure, my mother started dating this Jamaican guy, a U.P.S employee who also worked in Harlem. But how did Ethon know this? Easy. Because every move that my mother made, Ethon's niece would tell him. It was time for her to move out.

Unfortunately, she didn't move fast enough. One late summer afternoon as we sat outside on the steps taking in some fresh air, a large school bus slowly pulled up and stopped directly in front of the house.

"What's up?" It was the impostor himself.

"So 'dis is whaye all yuh lĭvin'?" he asked. In a way I was glad to see Teddy, but on the other hand, I couldn't stand the sight of his pale face.

"Hey Teddy! Did you sniff Nishi out?" my mother joked. A huge grin appeared on his face.

"Nah muhn - I wŭk (work) jus up dee street from haye. I pass haye be fo' and see dee vahn pa'hkd outside, but never saw you all," he explained.

"Oh okay." He and my mother carried on a conversation together for a few minutes.

"So Nishi whaye you been?" he asked while stepping off the bus.

"Some place where you haven't," I responded.

"I'm gonna go inside and let you two talk. So I guess I'll see you again huh Teddy, now that you know where we are?" My mother laughed and gathered her belongings.

"Yeah muhn." He smiled widely again. *I see the Clorox didn't work, so it is time to bring out the chisel.*

"Fuck off toe jam!" I mumbled when he reached for my hand.

"Nishi gyul, I love you so much and when I found out that you left, it hŭt (hurt) me bad muhn."

"Oh did it? The only thing that you missed was a piece of ass."

"I hate when you say stuff like that."

"Well it's the truth. Pussy is all you care about."

"No it's not," he argued.

"Oh no? Then why in the hell were two of your children born exactly two days apart from one another?"

"Where's Sara?" He changed the subject.

"Inside. Playing with Lee."

"Tell she that I will see she later."

"Later?" *Who invited him over?*

"Yeah later. I'll pass back later to see she. Let me go, I have to pa'hk dee bus up and clock out."

Twenty minutes later, a loud horn sounded. I looked through the window.

"Come Sara, let's go say hi to daddy!" I reached to pick her up.

"No. I don't wan-n-n-a!" She cried out.

"Come on!"

"No!" She snatched her hand back.

Obviously, this wasn't going to be easy, so I picked her up and carried her out. She scratched and screamed all the way to the front door.

"What's wrong wit she?" Teddy asked.

"She didn't want to come. I told her that we were coming to say hi to you and she flipped out."

"Ay-y-y-y! Gyul what's wrong wit (with) you?" he said, as he took her out of my arms.

Sara continued to scream and kick like a mad child.

"You want some cheeps (chips)?" he asked her.

"NO! LET ME GO!" She continued to kick and shout.

"Come. Let's go to de' sto' (the store)."

While holding her tightly, he jumped into his van and strapped her into the passenger seat.

"I'll be back," he said and drove off. I could hear Sara screaming throughout the van...

I waited outside thinking they'd be right back, but a nice amount of time passed by and still there was no sign of them. *I hope this fool did not take my baby around crazy ass MooMoo.* Rumor was she'd wanted a girl child too. I patiently sat on the concrete steps and finally his van turned the corner.

"Damn, it took you long enough! Where did you go?" I asked.

"We went to dee pa'hk (park)."

"Did you have fun baby?" I stooped to her level.

"Yes. I have chips Mommy!" she happily stated.

"I see! I see! He bought you some candy too huh? Wow! He spent a lot of money on his daughter today." I spoke sarcastically. She nodded her head yes, not understanding that I was disrespecting her father.

"Mommy can I go and show Lee?" Sara asked me.

"Yes, but be careful while going up those stairs okay." She quickly turned to run inside.

"Wait!" Teddy voiced. "Can I at least get a good-bye kiss?" Again Sara looked at him as if he were crazy.

"Gyul! You juss like you mudda (mother)," he pointed out. He picked her up, gently squeezed her and kissed her on the lips; this time she didn't cry.

"Nishi. I'm leaving. I'll see you around," he said.

"Whatever!" I went inside.

Now of course, my mother had something to say when he left.

"How nice! Daddy takin' his daughter out for a ride. Does this mean that you and Teddy are talking again?"

"Please. That brief visit meant nothing to me."

Two weeks later, we moved my mother out of that apartment.

"Mommy are you gonna pack your dishes and clothes in boxes?" I asked her.

"Nope. Just leave the clothes in the drawers and the dishes can go in those large garbage bags over there." She pointed out.

"But how will Rumps and his friend carry out that heavy chest of drawers?" I then asked.

"Well if they can't lift it, then tell them to take the drawers out," she advised while shoving the remaining of her belongings into a garbage bag. Being that Teddy had left for Grenada two days prior to her move, Rumps agreed to help us out with the use of Teddy's van.

"HOLD UP! HOLD UP!" I yelled as Rumps and his Rasta friend attempted to lower the chest down the last flight of stairs. "Her clothes are falling out!" I added.

Panties and all sorts of other shit had fallen out and to make matter's worse, an X-rated VHS tape had also fallen out and onto the ground. How embarrassing!

Not only did they now know the color of my mother's panties, but they also knew she was a freak. I quickly picked it up hoping that they hadn't seen the title, but it was too late. Chuckles came from both of them.

Even with both vans, we still made several trips before our move to Queens was complete. As Rumps and his friend carried up the last few pieces, I pulled my mother to the side.

"How much are you going to give them for helping you out?"

"Nish. You know that I don't have any money," she complained.

"Mommy! Are you serious?"

"Nishi, I have no money. If I have no money, then how am I going to give them something?"

"These are two grown men that carried your heavy furniture up and down several flights of stairs. You know what? Never mind. I'll give them something, but next time you need to be prepared!"

I gave Rumps fifty dollars and explained to him that this was all that I had and asked him if he was okay with it. He accepted the petty cash without a problem.

By the time Teddy returned to the states, we were somewhat relaxed in our new environment. It wasn't a mansion, but anything away from Ethon's family was good for my mother. Although I had passed all stages of The Dept. of Corrections hiring phase, unfortunately, they chose other candidates for the position. That was my final attempt to become a member of the law enforcement organization. I came to the conclusion that it wasn't meant for me.

Still desperately trying to do away with the welfare scene, I started working as a full- time temporary employee again. Sara was soon to be starting kindergarten and once again, I was starting to believe in myself. Realizing my strengths and weaknesses, I took on professional boxing lessons. This intense training was sure to keep me disciplined, physically fit and hopefully, one day competing in the Golden Gloves tournaments.

Every now and again Teddy would stop by and break up my concentration for a moment. He would hand deliver his infamous money orders and on occasion, we'd go out without Sara. The boxing thing must have been working because each time he came over, he'd compliment me on my physique.

As for my mother, she unfortunately attracted another asshole, but you couldn't tell her that he wasn't the catch of the month. Turns out this United Parcel employee was married with children and his wife was slowly catching on to his extra marital affair.

"What's up Nishi?" He spoke while visiting my mother one evening.

"Hey Bud!" I responded.

I had nicknamed him Bud because his eyeballs magnified through his thick eye wear, resembling the frog on the Budweiser commercial. It was obvious that he was another pussy hunter because on the very first day that I met him, he said something strange.

"When me finish wid (with) yuh mudda (your mother) she nah guh (won't) walk right."

Now how disrespectful was that? Each time he came over, they headed straight for her bedroom and closed the door. She claimed that he was giving her five hundred dollars per week. So what was she? The United States Postal Service second class whore? Please! All he did was stamp her and move on to his other packages...

_____

Shalon, my childhood friend who eventually became my motorcycle riding partner, remembered that I was seeking a full-time permanent position and informed me one day that her employer was hiring, but in a different department. I interviewed for the position and got the job.

"Now you can't give me some shit about you can't afford to buy another bike cause by next summer you should be straight. Your ass shouldn't have sold the other one in the first place," Shalon complained.

"Whatever ho!" I smiled.

The mere fact that I no longer owned a bike was eating me up inside. Some years after having Sara, I traded my bike for a car that I didn't keep for very long because I couldn't afford the auto insurance on it. Later, I found out that Shalon purchased a Yamaha 600 and couldn't believe it. When I had a bike, she didn't and now the situation was reversed. She claimed she wanted to surprise me, but turns out she was the one who was surprised.

Shalon was a good person with a touch of wilderness. I remember one night Shalon, Renee and myself attended a house party in Brooklyn. She must have been really thirsty cause she downed at least four Heinekens back to back.

"Nish pull up in that Wendy's please!" Shalon urgently requested.

"For what? They're closed," I responded.

"Yeah, the restaurant may be closed, but not the parking lot."

I pulled over so the drunkard could handle her business. She flung the door open and quickly squatted alongside the car.

"YOU BETTER DRIP DRY CAUSE THERE AIN'T NO TISSUE IN HERE!" I yelled out to her.

Why did a group of guys pull up shortly after Shalon crouched down? Slowly, I eased my foot off the brake pedal.

"NISH!" Shalon yelled while gripping the car door.

"What?" I casually looked back.

"WAIT! WHATCHU DOIN'?" she screamed as the car rolled away from her. With her panties down and her skirt raised above her knees, she held onto the door and hopped alongside the car to prevent the guys from seeing her.

"That'll teach you to drink so damn much!" I laughed.

"You're wrong Nish," Renee` chuckled.

I'll never forget that night and I'm sure Shalon won't either...

"Good morning Nishelle. This is Kelly, she'll be training you this week," the supervisor introduced us.

"Hello," I said as we shook hands.

"While you two get acquainted, I'll be at my desk finishing up some paperwork. Kelly show her around. Introduce her to the other girls!" The supervisor added.

"Is it Michelle or Nishelle?" Kelly asked.

"It's Nishelle," I responded as we entered a small room.

"Oh okay, so over here is our cafeteria; nothing fancy. And this is our computer room. Good morning Lorraine," Kelly greeted a passing co-worker.

"Oh Lorraine, this is Nishelle. She's new in our department. Nishelle, this is one of our computer technicians."

"No, you meant to say our best technician," Lorraine praised herself. *It never fails, there's always an asshole in every company.*

"Hello," I said to Lorraine.

"Hope you like it here," she responded and walked away.

"Okay, that's enough walking around. I'll introduce you to the others later," Kelly said and we returned to our department.

Later that evening, the wild child gave me a call.

"So Nish, how was your first day at work?"

"So far, so good." I said.

"Did you meet Charlene yet?" Shalon asked.

"Yeah. She seems cool."

"She's MAD cool. If you have any questions regarding an order just ask her because she knows her shit." Shalon explained.

"I also met this chic named Lorraine," I mentioned.

"Oh - from the computer room?"

"Yeah, she seems like a fuckin' snob," I was far from fond of this woman.

"Everybody says that when they first meet her, but she's cool. You just have to get to know her."

"Nah, that's alright. I'll pass."

"She's from Grenada too you know," Shalon informed me.

"Are you serious?" I frowned.

"Dead up!"

"Damn. Now I have to work with one of those small minded fucks too!" I grew disappointed.

"You're sick. Like I said once you get to know her she's cool peoples," Shalon reiterated.

"Whatever! Not if it came from Grenada," I concluded. "Anyway, are you riding to work tomorrow?"

"Probably. We're supposed to be having nice weather all week."

"Maybe I'll come and take a quick ride either on my lunch hour or before I go home," I told her.

"No problem. Damn, I'm here talking to you with this perm in my hair and it's starting to burn. Let me go and wash this shit out before I get soars all over my head. I'll see you tomorrow Nish."

"Okay - later."

Things were starting to pick up again. Now all I had to do was raise my daughter, focus on my training and open up a savings account.

"Mommy, school is about to start and we have to register the kids this coming Thursday," I reminded her.

"Damn!" she exclaimed. "The summer's over already?"

DING! DONG!

"Could that be my sweetie?" My mother ran to the door.

"Nope, it's for you Nishi," she said as she took a look through the peep hole then opened the door.

"What's up Teddy?" she greeted him.

"Hello – Goodnight," Teddy answered.

"SARA. YOUR DADDY'S HERE!" Lee yelled towards the back of the two bedroom apartment.

"Hey little muhn (man), what's up? Hi Nishi," Teddy greeted us.

"I see you're hanging out tonight. What happened - you and MooMoo had a fight?" I struck an argument. My mother smirked and exited the living room.

"Gyul, you talk so much shit," he said, shaking his head.

"I talk it! You're full of it! Wow – we're the perfect "mess." I thought you said that you were coming next Tuesday night?"

"Look gyul. I get haye when I get haye."

"YOU TELL HER TEDDY!" my mother screamed from her room.

"GLADYS YOU WANT A SMOKE?" he yelled back.

"SURE!" She quickly re-entered the living room.

"We at this shit again?" I frowned.

"It's only half a joint," Teddy declared.

"Idiot!" I uttered.

"You're gonna grow old fast if you don't watch it," my mother quipped.

"Yeah, the only thing that's gonna make me grow old is you two," I spat.

"What are you doing Saturday afternoon Teddy?" I changed the subject.

"Nothing really - why?"

"Because I want you to go with me somewhere," I replied.

"Okay," he agreed. That was easy!

After smoking the half joint with my mother, he laid across my lap and fell asleep. He left about two in the morning and later that afternoon Teddy, Sara and I went to Bedford Stuyvesant.

"Nishi – where are we going?" Teddy asked while driving.

"I'm going to see my father."

"Yeah? Have you spoken to him lately?" he asked.

"No. But I heard that he plays ball every weekend at the park on Bedford Avenue and Hancock Street. Make a left and park behind that Lincoln."

I took one deep breath and unlocked the door to get out.

"I'll be right back," I said.

While strolling through the park, I spotted his pale face running up and down the court.

"ROSS!" I yelled. He slowed down his dribble.

"ROSS!" I yelled again. He stopped and looked in my direction. "Can you come here please?" I politely asked him. From the look on his face he seemed unsure as to who I was, but still he slowly walked in my direction.

"Yes. May I help you?" He dragged his voice.

He and I stood at the same height. For the longest while, I was always curious to know which parent I really resembled. As a young child growing up I was always being told by the family that I looked, spoke and acted just like my father, but my mother's friends would say that I resembled her, which I ALWAYS denied. In my opinion, there was no resemblance between us two. My mother had a much darker complexion, a fat nose and HUGE teeth.

To add to my mental neglect, on occasion, my mother would tell me that I was adopted. Why would she even SAY something like THAT? I can only assume that negative memories of her old flame had entered her mind during those particular times.

Now having the opportunity to see my other half face to face gave me a chance to determine who I really looked like. He and I had the same fat chin, the same low hairline, straight noses, and the ability to raise our left eyebrow on impulse. The only dissimilarity was that I appeared to be about two shades darker than him. This felt weird.

"Do you have any idea who I am?" I asked Ross.

"No - No I don't." He slowly released his mindless statement. He had a very distinctive way of speaking.

"I'm Nishi - your daughter. You know Gladys right?"

"I don't know who you're talkin' about."

"You don't know Gladys?" I repeated the question, but in a deeper tone.

"No. No I don't. I'm sorry. Now will you excuse me?" He attempted to walk away.

"Wait a minute!" I stopped him. He and I both knew that he was lying.

"Well would you at least like to meet your granddaughter?" I asked him.

"How can I have a granddaughter when I don't even have a daughter?" WHAT!!!!!!!!

My heart dropped and at the same time I grew angry.

"You ain't nothin' but a tired ass drunk, and this you will always be."

I felt like punching him straight in his face, but instead I just said my piece and walked away. *How could he deny me like this?* I only wanted to talk and to introduce him to his granddaughter.

As I walked towards Teddy's van, so many thoughts and questions ran through my mind. *This must be a nightmare. My own father telling me HIMSELF that he doesn't have a daughter. Why can't things ever go right for me? I don't think I'm a bad person and yet, the negative always seems to clutch my soul.* God was punishing me forever because of the sins that I had committed back in my teen years.

"Nish! What happened? Was that him?" Teddy asked as I approached his van.

"Yeah. Let's go!" I said angrily.

It took me about a week before I mentioned me and Ross's very unpleasant and depressing conversation to anyone. Hoping that talking would heal the wound, I had a sit down with my aunt. She tried to convince me that my father was in denial and would feel it later, but for right now, I was the one feeling it.

What troubled me even more was I was beginning to see a trend. Like my father, Teddy wasn't too big on being a part of my daughter's life either. They were like violent storms; they'd make appearances to execute their damage and later disappear thoughtlessly.

Trying to make things clearer, Evelyn mentioned that it was a subconscious thing; me hooking up with Teddy. She believed I'd fallen in love with him because he so very much resembled Ross. She also inferred that I was lacking the love and attention of my father to the point where I convinced myself that Teddy could fill that gap. One thing's for certain, my life was a tsunami of drama.

Teddy tried everything to lift my spirits. We went out to dinner, joined some friends at a backyard gathering and even went to the theater to see a movie, but despite his efforts nothing aided my pain. I desperately just wanted to be left alone.

"Who in here is havin' a baby?" my little brother asked as he entered the living room one evening.

"What?" I asked as I began to laugh. This kid was too much for me.

"I said, who's havin' a baby? Who left this E.P.T. wrapper in the bathroom?" My little brother awaited an answer. All I could do was laugh.

"Maybe me - I don't know," I toyed with him a little.

"We gonna get another Sara? That little girl's bad," Lee stated seriously.

"I think it's time for you to find your own apartment Nishi, because this place ain't big enough for all of us and Shadow," the little punk added.

Shadow was our German Sheppard mixed puppy we adopted from the North Shore Animal League just months after moving into that apartment.

"Shut up you midget!" I popped him on his head.

"And I hope this one's a boy," Teddy said as he held me from behind while we stood in the kitchen.

"Yeah?" I smiled.

"For real! Then we would have the perfect pair," he added.

"True," I cooed.

"I love you so much Nishi," Teddy softly whispered in my ear. "I could marry you right now."

That's all I needed to hear. Instantly, I turned and faced him.

"Are you serious?" My mind was no longer in idle mode.

"Yeah!" He hugged me tighter than ever.

From his hug alone, I felt that he was serious, but I had to make sure. I took a step back to gap our bodies and looked directly into his eyes.

"Seriously, are you serious?" I asked again. He smiled and kissed my forehead.

"When can we do it? And let me just tell you now - I don't want a City Hall wedding either!" I pushed the topic. Teddy rejoined our bodies, but his silence confused me.

"I'm kiddin'," he smiled.

"What?" I scowled.

"I'm just kiddin' gyul," he repeated.

"Get the hell off of me!" I pushed him away. And to think, for a moment there, I was on top of the world...

"THE TRUTH SHALL SET US FREE!"

WE WILL ALWAYS BE TOGETHER I CAN FEEL IT IN

MY HEART

WE'LL EXCHANGE THOSE VOWS TIL DEATH DO

US PART

FREE! FREE! FREE! LIKE A BIRD

IT'S TIME TO TELL THEM AND LET OUR LOVE BE

HEARD

"Hey biker chic what's up?" Shalon stopped by my department one afternoon.

"Hey, what are you doing over here - messin' around?" I asked her.

"Nah. I'm on my lunch."

"Oh, okay."

"Girl, this morning I was running late. You should have seen me. I had to finish my hair."

"Your hair?" I asked.

"Yeah. Last night I put some tracks in the back of my head but I couldn't do the front 'cause I ran out of glue, so this morning I ran to the hair supply shop, ran back home and glued the rest of this shit to my head in a hurry."

"It looks fine to me. I can't tell that you rushed it."

"Please. I got glue all over the place tryin' to hurry up," Shalon chuckled.

"Girl. I have something to tell you!" I said.

She turned her head and looked at me from the corner of her eye.

"I know what it is!" she said, sucking her teeth.

"No you don't."

"Yes I do, your ass is pregnant again." Shalon hit the nail on its head. "Nishi, from the moment you said, I have to tell you something. I knew what it was. What else could it be? That's all you and Teddy know how to do is make babies," she laughed.

"Fuck you and your maple tree legs. Ever since I've known you, your thighs and ankles have always been the same size. You need to take some water pills or stop eatin' all that damn pork," I joked.

"Shut up Nishi! Now you got my stomach hurting from laughing too hard."

"It's not me has your stomach hurting, it's that freakin' pork and besides having a baby is exactly what you need."

"Oh yeah and why is that?" she queried.

"Cause then maybe you'll stop having those painful ass periods every month," I pointed out.

"Nah - that's alright. I'll leave the baby making up to you."

"Whatever! Don't wait 'til it's too late. Damn baby might come out with eight arms. One for every glass of Hennessey and Coke `cause his mama ain't nothin' but a damn alcoholic. At parties dancing on the tables and shit. Embarrassing my ass like that – just makes no sense."

"You're stupid Nish." She was now laughing harder now.

"Well, I guess there goes your motorcycle next summer," she said, rubbing it in.

"Shalon. is your lunch over yet?" I rolled my eyes at her.

"Nope!" she laughed. "I still have thirty minutes left."

Lorraine walked up just as she was saying this.

"I can't believe this! You walked three entire blocks to get here, yet you didn't even bother to come and say hello to me, the most educated employee at this company!" Lorraine stated in a very cocky tone as she approached me and Shalon.

"Shut up you book worm! I was going to right after talking to Nishi. But now that you're over here, I can save a trip," Shalon joked.

"You two met one another right?" Shalon asked us both.

"Yeah we've met," I muttered. *UNFORTUNATELY!* This woman was so annoying.

"Lorraine, Nishi's boyfriend is also from Grenada," Shalon announced.

"Yeah. What's his name? I might know him," Lorraine asked me.

"I doubt it," I said trying to cut the conversation short.

"Sweetheart, Grenada is a very small country, so believe me. I may know him."

"His name's Teddy." I threw his name out there.

"Teddy. No, I don't know any Teddy's. What's his last name?" Lorraine dug deeper.

"Ruthbun."

"Nope. Still doesn't ring a bell. How does he look?" Lorraine continued to interrogate me. *Damn bitch, leave it the hell alone already!*

"Forget it cause you don't know him," I said with somewhat of an attitude, hoping she'd get the hint.

"Well ladies, it's been grand. I have fifteen minutes left to my lunch hour and I wanna make a quick stop at Mickey Dee's. Talk to y'all later."

"Alright," I said.

"So how does he look?" Lorraine eagerly asked, picking up right from where she had left off.

For a moment I sat looking away. This damn woman wants me to snap on her ass.

"He's tall, slim and light skinned with hazel eyes."

"He has one brother right?" Lorraine seemed to be on to something.

"Yeah," I said.

"Does he have curly hair and drives a big van?" *Wait! Could this bougie bitch really know him?*

"Yeah," I answered.

"I know him!" She stood on her feet and widened her eyes. "Well, I don't know him like that, but I know of him. He and his brother look alike and they live in those buildings right off of Empire Boulevard. Yeah, I know him. A pack of fuckin' Indians live in those buildings up there."

I sat quietly at my desk as she rambled on.

"But that's a married man," she stated.

"He's not married," I responded while looking dead at her.

"Oh YES he is! His wife went to school with my sister back home. They've been married for some time now and she has two sons for him. I was invited to the wedding, but I didn't go because I had a prior engagement. Plus, I don't really know them both like that."

You could have fooled me. I clenched my teeth.

"Well let me go," she said and walked her funny shaped ass out of my department.

"Black bitch." I mumbled to myself...

As the weeks emerged into a new month, I grew angrier and angrier. We were once again approaching the holidays and this year instead of staying home with the family, my mother and Lee were going to Jamaica with Bud.

"Nishi, I just wanna remind you that we have to be at the airport by 5:00 in the morning," my mother said all pumped up and ready to go.

"What time is the plane leaving?" I asked.

"It leaves at 6:00, but I wanna be there AT 5:00."

"OKAY. I heard you the first time."

For many years, I hadn't used my inhaler, but for some reason I felt the urge to use it now. Worried that the asthma medication could harm the baby, I called my obstetrician.

"Hi. This is Nishelle Maron. Is it possible that I could speak with Dr. Obanka?"

"He's with a patient right now, but I could take a message and have him call you when he becomes available," the woman suggested.

"Okay - that's fine," I said.

"Are you pregnant?"

"Yes."

"How far long are you?" the woman asked.

"A little over three months."

"Okay. And are you having any problems?"

"Yes. I have asthma and for these past couple of weeks I've been having a hard time breathing," I explained.

"And you wanna know if you can use your inhaler - right?" The woman knew my next question.

"Yeah - how did you know?"

"Because you're like the third pregnant patient that has called with the same problem this week," she stated.

"It's this weather," I said but in my case, I knew it was this man.

Asthma is not only triggered by physical exertion or environmental changes, it can also flare up simply from escalated stress levels.

"I'm sure he'll say that you can use it, but to be on the safe side let's wait until he gives you a call back."

"Thanks," I appreciated her assistance.

"You're quite welcome and you have a good night."

"Thank you... you too."

Due to the fact the holidays were here again, I knew that my chances of seeing Teddy were very slim. Although, I hadn't spoken to him about this so called marriage yet, the deep rooted anger gradually faded. I promised myself that I'd remain calm until I found out the real deal.

RING! RING!

"Hello," I answered.

"Hey! Whucha doin'?" It was Grams.

"Peeling potatoes so I could start this potato salad that you asked me to bring for Thanksgiving."

"Did you finish the cake yet?" she asked.

"Yeah. I just have to decorate it though."

"So what time are you gonna be here tomorrow?"

"I don't know. I guess about two or three o'clock."

"Two or three o'clock! That's mighty late Nishi. I was wondering if you could pick up mother on your way here."

"Fine!" I sighed. "Just make sure she's ready, cause I'm not tryin' to smell her bucket."

DING! DONG!

"Grams - hold on okay? Someone's at the door." I laid the receiver down. It was Teddy.

After letting him in, I continued with my telephone conversation while he played with Sara in the living room.

"Yeah Grams I'm back."

"Who is it?" She asked.

"Teddy."

"Oh so you have company now? Tell him that I said hello and I'll talk to you tomorrow."

"Okay, I will. Bye," I said and hung up the phone. I didn't want to cut Sara's most memorable moment with her father, so I continued to peel the rest of the potatoes.

At about ten o'clock that night, I prepared Sara for bed.

"Sara it's time to go to bed."

"I wanna stay with you," she whined.

"No. It's late. Don't you wanna see Juju and the rest of your cousins tomorrow?"

"Yes," she frowned.

"Okay, then let's go to bed so you can get a good night's rest."

"No!" She squeezed between her father and me on the couch.

"Move! This is my Mommy!" She shoved him.

"Ay-y-y-y! Who you pooshin' (pushing) gyul?" Teddy grabbed hold of her hands.

"Let me go!" She lowered her head and tried to bite him on his leg.

"Okay! Okay! I'm let'ten (letting) you go. Chuh muhn – dis gyul is just like she mudda," he frowned at me.

"Whatever!" *If only you knew..this is only the beginning of tonight's episode.* In order for Sara to fully drop asleep, I had to lay down with her for a while.

"So, are you going to ask me if I like my new job or not?" I asked upon returning to the living room

"Do you like your new job Nishi?"

"Yeah. It's alright, but the crowded train rides suck."

"Well, I'm sure people will soon give up their seats once you start showing," he laughed.

"Mmm, I doubt it," I said.

Slowly, Teddy slid his hand up my shirt and rubbed my belly.

"So uhhhh...do you know someone by the name of Lorraine?" I asked him.

"Nuh Uh!" He shook his head, continuing to stare at the television.

"She's from Grenada. A slim dark skinned girl with a high butt," I described.

He pretended to be engrossed by whatever show that was on at the time.

"TEDDY!" I shouted. "Do you hear me talkin' to you?" I pushed his hand away.

"What's wrong wit you gyul?" he snapped. "I told you I don't know a Lorraine from back home."

"Well she claims that she knows you."

"That's she business."

"Are you married?" I got straight to the point.

"Nishi what's wrong wit you?" he frowned.

"What do you mean what's wrong with me? I'm just asking you a simple question. ARE - YOU - MARRIED?"

"We at this shit again?" He grew annoyed.

"It's a simple yes or no answer." I added some pressure. He sat upright and reached for his shoes.

"What are you doing? Are you leaving now?" I asked him.

"Gyul, just leave me alone cause you're talkin' foolishness."

"Oh am I? Well Ms. Lorraine claims you and MooMoo have been married for quite some time now and she also mentioned your two sons."

"Nishi, call me when you stop wit you shit." He opened the door and exited the apartment.

"Whatever!"

Returning to work from an extended weekend was of course, undesirable because (1) you can never get enough rest and (2) I had to spend 1/3 of my day with a flippin' stranger that had thorough knowledge of my messed up love life.

"Good morning Nishelle. How was your Thanksgiving?" Lorraine asked.

"Pretty good and yours?" I responded.

"It went well but you know what I meant to ask you?"

"What?" I asked in a crude manner. Her inappropriate interrogations annoyed me like hell.

"Are you the same Nishi that had a baby for him?"

It was time for me to put this bitch in her place. Her severe case of diarrhea of the mouth had to be constipated.

"Look! You obviously have no life and I'd appreciate it if you'd stop with the questions," I warned her.

"I just wanted to know, because the Nishi that I heard about has locks," she said, completely ignoring me.

"I think you need to get out of my face right now because you're starting to get on my nerves."

"What are you snapping at me for? Shit, I'm not the one who's dealing with a married man."

This bitch was most definitely looking for a beat down. With my left eyebrow raised, I looked up at her.

"You are fuckin' with the wrong person!"

"You know what, act like this conversation never happened." She withdrew herself from the discussion and spun on her cheap ass looking shoes. Only 9:30 in the morning and my day was already screwed up...

On the way home that evening, I wondered how I was going to pull through this one. My mother had been home for two days now and the last thing that I wanted to do was overwhelm her with my problems. Especially since Bud's wife was now calling the apartment after establishing that her husband was accompanied by a female companion in Jamaica. The sex crazed Bud neglected to remove the hotel receipt from his pants pocket, which had all of my mother's information on it. The Mrs. no longer had to question her husband's infidelity; it was all in writing.

"Hello," Lee answered. But after the hello I didn't hear him say anything else. He simply hung up.

"Lee who was that on the phone?" my mother asked her young son.

"I don't know, some lady. She said to tell you to leave other people's husbands alone."

The Mrs. was no joke; several months later she left him with a mortgage and a microwave to cook his food in. Just imagine how his big eyes bulged when he entered his house to find his family and everything gone. What a big "FUCK YOU" that must have been.

"Mommy?" I knocked on her closed door.

"What is it'?" she asked.

"Are you busy? Can I talk to you for a minute?"

"Yeah!" she replied. I pushed open the door and leaned up against her dresser. She turned down the T.V. and gave me her undivided attention.

"Mr. Teddy's married!" I stated.

"Who says?" she quickly responded.

"Coincidentally, some chick that I work with knows him and everything about him."

"But how did she find out that you two knew one another?"

"Shalon mentioned to her that my boyfriend was also from Grenada during one of our conversations at work."

"Oh, so this girl's from Grenada too?" my mother asked, putting two and two together.

"Yep! Anyway, she told me everything."

"Well do you believe her?"

"Yeah because I asked him."

"And what did he say?"

"Nothin' as usual. But after I kept bugging him about it, he told me to stop talking foolishness and then he left."

"Oh, but he never really admitted to it though?"

"Mommy please! When a person tries to or avoids a simple YES or NO question, what else is there for me to believe."

"True - true."

"Plus, he was relaxed. Stretched out on the couch with his shirt and shoes off, watchin' T.V. and then all of a sudden he jumps up and starts gettin' dressed. Seriously, if that ain't an admission then what is it?"

"So when did all of this take place?" she inquired.

"While you were in Jamaica."

"Oh well," was all she said. There were times when I regretted talking to my mother and this was definitely one of them.

"Well, I have something to tell you too," she said in her "better luck next time" tone of voice. Her careless attitude made me want to leave her room, but I simply stood there waiting for her to break me down even more.

"I'm pregnant too!" she vibrantly stated.

"For real? How many weeks are you?" I was happy for her.

Another baby was something that she obviously wanted because this was her third pregnancy within the last two years.

"I'm four months," she answered.

"Four months?" I asked surprisingly.

"Yep!" She displayed those huge enamel choppers of hers.

"Why didn't you say anything? You mean to tell me that we're going to have our babies a month apart?"

"Just about, and the reason that I didn't say anything to anyone is because I haven't had much luck in the past."

"That's understandable. So what did the doctor say? Is everything alright so far?"

"Well, my next appointment is in two weeks, but so far – so good," my mother smiled.

Lee was right. This place wasn't big enough for all of us...

It took him some time but Teddy finally admitted to the marriage. This of course, didn't sit well with me and following his confession, I asked him why? His response was that her father was dying and his last wish was to see his youngest daughter married, which most likely was another one of his tall tales.

Enough of this madness! I have cried too many tears and listened to too many of his lies. And for what? When was it going to stop? When am I going to put my foot down and say ENOUGH...

ABOUT THE AUTHOR

Author Nichole Martin resides in New York state with her family and is a serious Domestic Violence/Abuse Advocate.

VM3: Headed Str8t 4 TROUBLE is the third installment in her Venomous Minds Series and is based on a true story.

Make sure you check out VM1: The First Bite is the Deepest &

VM2: Poison Running Free

You can find these great titles on Amazon.com and on the author's website:

www.smilesforthefuture1.com/